WHISPERS FROM THE DEAD OF NIGHT

Lee Allen

For Grandad, who went out into the night too soon.

CONTENTS

A DEATHLY

I am amongst the fragmented, like I an.

unknown quantity no longer wholly me, ground to dust and dispersed like slivers of shattered glass, carried as the breeze carries grains across dunes of sand, far and wide and without their own defined and fixed space, without their own identity. Is it possible that in those pieces are parts of me now irretrievable, like an emotion no longer felt, a memory without recollection, a lesson unlearned? Has the whole of me – my body, my mind, my soul – become so unrecognisable that I am no longer myself; that whatever I feel that I am, is simply not, and I am only a single fragment, drifting in desolation and bewilderment, like that single grain of sand, until it snuffs out like dispelled smoke, as all other fragments have been or will soon follow?

Consciousness thuds into my brain, hammering at my skull with relentless malice, daring the fog clouding my mind to clear, to burn my retinas with the truth of clarity. In this fog floats the remaining pieces of me, in a cloud of dislocation. The pain sears through my head, ringing down my ear canals, breath catching in my throat as if taken for the first time. Light-headedness is like a hot, clammy hand clasping my brain, sucking me down into a vacuum.

Vision blurred; I am aware only of the cold. My fingertips feel enclosed in icicles, breeze ruffling the hairs on my hands with a coating of moisture. I startle, rising quickly, and realise how stiff my body has become, collapsing back and hitting solid ground – yet feel it sway beneath me. A wave of disorientation, like the cloud has formed a fist with which to break me down; I raise my arms to protect my face from the blows. But they do not come. My breathing sounds shallow to my ears, alien and not from my own body, part of the tapestry of the looming threat that does not manifest, but simply hovers, its shadow a constant and lingering spectre.

I drop my arms, hearing the splash as my fingertips collide with the iciness once more. Only now does clarity break a small dawn into my consciousness; I am beside water, my cold hand and arm the victim of its selfish kisses. I pull my hand away, reaching instinctively to wipe away the water on my coat. I stroke the fleece lining, its thick durability, understanding now why only parts of my body feel the chill, others insulated. Fragmented awareness.

My movements have triggered nerve endings to send sluggish messages to my brain, the burning crick in my neck forcing its way through the laziness, demanding to be acknowledged. I am slouched into a corner and my hand moves from my coat to what lies beneath me. It is solid, neither the soft sand nor rough earth I had expected. It is smooth, not the rugged formation of rock. My skin catches, pierced, blood drawn. A splinter. I am on a wooden surface. I force my body upward to relieve the pain, the ground rocking, my hand gripping an edge beyond which is thickening fog. I am on a boat, a small wooden boat in a sea of mist.

I listen to the silence, staring into the blackened water and the thick blanket of grey that hovers above it. I can see no more than a few feet beyond the edge. I watch the impenetrable blackness of the water and wonder at what is lurking just beneath the surface, that if my hand were to break the rippling calm if I would be dragged from where I sit. In the dark, there is no indication of the water's depth or the dangers it obscures. By night, it is a great slumbering beast that when awakened will erupt with hisses and roars. But for now, its sound is silence, but for the lapping at the sides of the boat, the gentle breathing of sleep.

I cannot remember how I came to be here, what led me to set off from the shore, nor even how far away that may be. I crane my sore neck, only to see more fog thickening in my vision, the black water beyond the stern of the wooden vessel. I climb to my feet carefully, slowly, the boat rocking with my movements. I grip the side as I stand, stooping, praying I will not be tipped over into the murky depths. As I steady myself, I pull my coat tight around me, squinting into the fog. There is nothing to see.

I register movement to my left. From the little I see, it cannot be a large boat on which I find myself, suggesting the movement is at its bow. I hear dragging in the water, subtle under the constant lapping against wood. Again, my eyes detect movement, a flash of ivory dim amongst the fog.

"Hello?" My voice cracks in my throat, the words escaping in a hoarse whisper. I clear my throat soundlessly, now unsure whether I ought to call out again.

Beneath the swell of the water, I hear the ripple of musical notes, incongruous in this cavern of mist and water. It is far away, a glimpse of the land I left behind or a memory I can't quite reach out and hold, I cannot be sure which. No longer am I stood on the deck; I dance, swirling in circles, no longer in my heavy lined coat, dressed in tails, my partner nestled in my arms, as elegant as she is beautiful. My hand reaches to touch her face, but she is gone, disintegrating into mist, her image now unclear in my mind.

The boat rocks with my loss of concentration, my body unbalanced. I shift my feet to steady myself, aware again of movement at the bow.

"Hello?" I call again, bravery taking hold of me from I know not where. "Where are we?"

There is no reply, nor do I expect one. Whomever is ferrying me across this expanse of water in the darkest hour of the night, they have no intention of making themselves known. Were I a braver man, perhaps I would tackle them in the darkness and row the boat myself to safety. But where is safety? Furthermore, am I not more likely to capsize the boat and send us both into the icy depths? I wouldn't bet against the chances of survival in these waters being short, that taking no consideration for what may be brought to the surface to investigate such a commotion as two fighting people and a damaged, sinking rowing boat.

The wind picks up, blowing moisture into my face. Wiping my nose and forehead, I am surprised at the crinkled paper touch of my skin and squint at my hands as I hold them to my face. They are the hands of an old and weathered man. Could I have forgotten growing old? What happened to the intervening years between this moment and the young man dancing with his bride?

Bride? The woman with the beautiful face whom I cannot quite remember – could she really be my wife? I am no longer a young man, but I am sure I have never been a beautiful one. Am I simply an old and lost soul dreaming of chances I never had? I do not remember my advancing years, but I cannot be sure that the woman I cannot clearly see, who fills my heart with a swelling I cannot fathom as I speculate on what I cannot recollect, is any more solid a memory than the years that are as fluid and spectral as the mist I must surely be cutting through as we progress so slowly across this blackened expanse that I cannot be sure the boat is moving at all.

Fatigue burns in my bones and I squeeze my eyes shut. The wind and my faltering balance create a precarious rocking. I am already far too cold and weak to risk a plunge into the depths. Were my companion to help me to safety, I cannot be sure that the result would be a positive one. Perhaps sinking ever deeper into the blackness to meet the unknown would be a relief, a rescue from the unknown trials of the future.

I gratefully sink to the stern once more, the hard edges harsh through my coat. I squeeze the pins and needles from my fingers with the fingers of my other hand alternately, hoping to squeeze blood back into them to fight out the chill.

I listen to the distant stillness, the wash of the water as the wooden vessel cuts through it inch by inch, the insistent splash of the oar, my companion's heavy silence mere feet from me.

Why did she leave me?

The thought stabs through my pondering, accompanied by a lightness in my head and a heaviness in my chest that have me convinced I will expire here on the deck, relieving my companion of whatever need they have for me. Who left me? The woman with the simultaneously beautiful and featureless face?

Was I not enough? Have I failed her? Did I not support her in times of strife and suffering, or celebrate her at times of peace and happiness? Have I broken my vows? I am convinced I have failed her deeply, that I must have done. I miss her dreadfully.

For a fleeting moment, there was a glimpse of clarity, but now it is again gone, drifting away on the mist, driftwood on the murky waters.

I hear the persistent swish of the oar, determined, unrelenting, driven by the hand of someone who cannot be more than two yards away from me, obscured in the mist that prevents me seeing more than a few feet ahead. Questions spin around my mind, unaided by memory. Captor or rescuer, I cannot know. I am tempted to call out, to ask who they are, but am struck dumb by my conviction that ignorance is favourable, that they wish to do me harm.

How did I come to be here? If I could reach out to that fragment and pluck it from the wilderness of thoughts and emotions, I may be able to solve the mystery of my kidnapper's identity, so silent beyond the reach of my vision. The music I heard may have been from distant land, where I was attacked and subdued while I took a break from the dancing and celebrations. Yet that cannot be a recent memory, unless I have aged some fifty or sixty years during our journey.

I grip my head in my fingers, desperate to squeeze some sense, some memory, from the grey matter inside my skull. I have no strength in my fingers, the sensation weak and fruitless. I feel like screaming. What use am I to myself if I cannot form a coherent memory, cannot logically process what lies before me? My mind is a fog, much like the green-grey mist thickening around me.

Movement beside the boat captures my attention, a shape beneath the water, a darkening of the oily surface. I lean over, careful not to put too much weight to one side of the boat. Yet my small movements have little impact while my body is prostrate. My strength has long since departed, the weight of a strong, young man now degenerated to skin and bone and gristle, barely able to match the impact of a feather. To trouble this vessel, I must stand and move wildly, forget my balance as I cry out into the night.

I watch the water. The shape is getting closer. What can be worse? A monster of the deep or the captor who remains silent in the dark? I draw back, the shape rising. It breaks the surface, water running in rivulets from its face. It is her; unblemished, alabaster skin. She floats on the surface, eyes and lips closed. I reach a trembling hand over the edge of the boat, mist tendrils of smoke around my skin. My thin fingers feel as if they could snap in the frigid air.

If only I can touch her, perhaps I will remember.

She sinks from my fingertips, swallowed by the inky waves.

"No!"

I lunge to grab hold of her. My hand cups only water, the boat rocking.

Thunder growls in the distance.

"Who are you?" I cry into the fury, unsure if I am asking the question of the woman beneath the surface or whomever is at the helm of the boat. Yet neither answer.

In spite of myself I begin to weep, despair and isolation gripping my heart. Dry, soundless sobs tremble my weak, cold body. The thunder gives it its voice, a mighty roar that my lungs could no longer support.

Somewhere beneath it, there is a whispering, as quiet but persistent as the dripping of a tap. Barely audible, but I detect it as a voice, as her voice.

The hardest thing was leaving you.

Lightning tears the fog to shards, allowing me a glimpse beyond its shroud. Water, seemingly for miles; water, cloud and emerald sky as one, silhouetted against it a figure in a hooded cloak, brandishing an oar; before again only the misty dark, with hues of green and grey.

I watch the heavy veil, thunder rumbling.

Rain pierces the fog, delivering powerful blows, slashing through the shroud that covers the water and the small boat. The raindrops are harsh and brutal, stinging my eyes and skin. I shield my face with an arm, trying to push myself to a sitting position with my other arm, finding I do not have the strength.

Lightning sets the world ablaze once more, veiled in a ghostly green, a concoction of the storm's blue light against the red of a setting sun. But has the sun not long since set? How could I know, lost in this fog? The deck is fully visible in these few seconds. The hooded figure is turning to face me, its face obscured, before I return to the dark.

The rain is freezing to hail, cutting at my hands and face. I feel my cheek tear, blood joining the ice-cold water running down my face and neck. The boat moves rapidly, rocked back and forth by the might of the ocean, water spilling over the edges from the waves. The excited current pulls the boat in differing directions, spinning clockwise, then anti-clockwise. I cling to the edge, unable to distinguish between the roars of the waves, the thunder and the hail.

Lightning illuminates the deck on which I lie, helpless, hopeless, simultaneous with a booming eruption that must be the thunder beyond the crazed fury of the water. The cloaked figure steps closer. I can neither move nor make a sound as vision vanishes. How can this creature maintain its balance? The boat spins, tipping, water pooling at my back, my feet submerged. I am sure that my captor will finally be lost, pulled from the deck into the swirling currents below.

The sky tears open once again. The figure looms over me, a hand outstretched towards me.

Finally, I scream, the boat lurching as I feel bony fingers close around my face. I struggle, just as a wave hits the edge of the boat, tipping me to the left. I hold on to the edge tightly, convinced we are about to capsize, but the tiny vessel lurches back, counterbalancing against the force, tipping to the right. My hold is dislodged. I pour into the water, immediately submerged, flailing arms and legs. My mouth opens and I taste salt and sand, spluttering and gulping more. My chest burns. I feel my body sinking, the weight of the water above me, pushing me deeper.

Shapes move beneath me, hungry, awaiting their prey. Slave to the water, I am dragged around like a child's lost toy. I break the surface, clawing breath into my ragged throat. All I feel are needles, cutting and tearing my body from the inside out. I see nothing, not the boat, not even the sky above me. Another wave rises over my head.

My arms are weakening, barely able to move. Final pockets of air escape my screaming mouth. My bones are lead, sinking through the water, away from where the current commands and goes to war with the raging air.

She is here, sinking with me. I have barely the strength in my fingers as she reaches for my hand, her face floating mere inches from my own. A single bubble escapes her lips and she giggles, girlish, but I cannot hear anything but water. Her hair rises above her head, drifting around her. Weight pulls on my feet and I wonder how far there is to sink. Perhaps the sinking is endless.

She speaks, but I cannot hear her. I reach for her other hand, but cannot find it. She blinks sadly, as if she is crying, but I cannot see her tears beneath the water. I close my eyes, trying to squeeze out the sting, so that I can see clearly the words which she speaks.

It was never my intention to cause you so much pain.

Something hits me from behind, a crushing blow to my spine that catapults me forward, spinning over her head. The current takes a grip on me again, a whirlpool somersaulting my body, vision lost in a rush of water and sand, salt stinging my lips and eyes. Punched and kicked, I am sure that my bones will snap, that my useless, weak body can endure no more.

Finally, I crush against solid ground, exhausted, drained of all I have left. Have I reached the sea bed? Or have I found my place between a rock crevice, trapped there for the water to assault me anew?

The thundering begins to dissipate. Fluid drains from my ears. The storm has passed, the ocean calming. Is this the sound of death?

Fog has filled my head, obscuring the last shards of my splintered mind. My body feels heavy. I try to move and cannot. I no longer know my own body – estranged; it has betrayed me along with my mind. There was a time I felt in control of both; they were part of me, an extension of me, synchronised. Now I cannot trust what either do, for they do not bend to my will.

The ground beneath me is cold and damp. It feels like grit in my slashed cheek, stinging with salt. I am able to move my fingers, clumps of sludge forming beneath my hands. My limbs rest at unnatural angles. The water is behind me. I bend my elbow, bend my wrist, prop a palm flat on the ground. It sinks as I push against it. I bend a knee, feel a rock sharp against my kneecap. I bend another knee and stagger back, still pushing with my hand, splashing back into the water as I look around and above me.

I find myself on a beach, dark, derelict. I may have been here for hours on the sand, I cannot know. The sea spat me out. I look behind me, the shimmering blackness, fog hanging low over the water. I cannot see a boat, no battered carcass of one floating to shore.

I look along the beach. The mist does not hang so heavily over the land. The grey sand runs smoothly in both directions, black hulks of trees looming beyond it. Rocks frame the sand on either side, no more than shapes that could easily be cloaked and hooded figures awaiting my next move. I get to my feet, legs stiff and crooked, staggering forward, only just saving myself from falling to the sand. I am unsure if I could get back up again, I have so little energy.

It is damp and cold, biting wind riding in from the sea. I turn towards it, then the trees, then into the distance to the rocks, unable to shake off my bewilderment. Far from the dancing and the laughter and the youthful woman; they are all dimmed now, like an old photograph in sepia you cannot remember being taken. My shoulders sag. I do not truly have options when I cannot know where any of them may lead me.

So, I simply choose to turn right and begin to trudge in that direction, following the line of the sea, sand slopping beneath my feet. Slow already, I am slowing more. I move up the sand a little, away from the water, which is again beginning to grow agitated. The rocks loom larger with my painful progress. I still see the fleshless hand reaching for me from beneath the cloak.

I should stop, to take the weight off my sore feet, to calm the tightness in my chest. I cough and gag, still tasting saltwater. Head down, stumbling, I know I must soon stop before I collapse here and rot from exposure, unless the sea reaches out to take me back beforehand. I need heat, I need shelter. I look to the trees, ominous strangers, knowing they are my final hope.

I look around the sand at my feet, searching for pebbles. The beach is strewn with them, cast up the shore by the cantankerous tides. I stoop to investigate them closely, hearing my knees and back crack in protest. I find a sharp-edged stone, suitable for stripping and sanding wood. With my pebble clasped in my palm, I look to the trees with some trepidation. Behind any of the gnarled trunks that merge with ease into the shadows could lurk my hooded companion from the boat. But he could not have survived.

Yet somehow you *did.*

I turn to look back to the shore. It is her voice; I am sure of it. But I can see no one, nor hear anything more, only the swell of the waves, now the gentle snoring of a slumbering beast.

I search for tinder amongst the shrubbery and the low-hanging branches, thankful that the tide does not appear to reach this far, as the ground is dry. I scrape the brittle moss from the trunks of trees with the pebble, chipping off the dead bark, gathering it with fallen leaves and small twigs that have gathered on the ground. My coat is sodden, unsuitable for keeping my bundle dry, so I feel around in the earth, having to abandon my tinder.

I stumble and trip, each time feeling a new pain or twinge in my body. I do not know it still – it has forsaken me, no longer working in harmony with my mind.

Rummaging in the undergrowth for some time, I find a large, flat rock, its top smooth as slate, scraping dry earth from it victoriously. It takes a great will of strength to lift it, fatigue deep to the bone in my arms. With the rock in both my hands, I return to the base of the tree I began with, gathering up my tinder and collecting it atop my find.

I feel above my head for snags and test the ends of branches. These trees are dead. I estimate the season as late autumn or winter, accounting for how cold I am in this wilderness. I wonder how I spent the last summer, indeed all my summers, dreaming at the notion of a summer evening dancing. Did I make her laugh? Did her heart sing and her stomach flutter in my presence?

I scold myself. I am an old man, thinking a young man's thoughts. But when do we realise we have grown old? Is it the day our bodies begin to let us down? I wish I could remember when I first felt it. Aging is not an abrupt new phase, but a gradual realisation. Perhaps it took me years, to wake one morning with the acceptance that I was no longer young, that despite my mind feeling and thinking the same, my body has slowly committed its act of treachery, unwilling to fight nature in the way my mind is capable.

My kindling gathered on the ground beside my rock of tinder, I search for larger dead branches. Carrying branches under my arms, I return to the beach, choosing a spot only a few feet from the trees, hoping for adequate shelter from the wind. I place my palm flat on the sand, checking that it is dry. I return to the trees for the tinder and kindling. I squint into the distance, but only blackness sways there.

Sitting on the sand, I claw out a small pit in front of me, hoping this will defeat the breeze. I choose the three largest branches and prop them around the hole, pushing them into the sand for foundation, all three meeting at the top, wedged together. Smaller branches prop against and inside the cone.

From the rock I take the mix of bark and leaves, moulding them together with my fingers into a small ball with an indent in its centre. I lace the stems of leaves to hold it together, combatting the lifeless fragility. The remainder of the tinder I scoop into the hole beneath the cone.

I pause, looking out to sea. Where did I come from? Where am I going? Perhaps the most crucial question: will that be different to the destination my captor intended, or am I on an inevitable course?

I begin work on the two branches I have kept aside, concentration distracting and focussing my disjointed mind. With the sharp pebble, I gouge a hole out of the flatter branch, having to lean over it to put my weight behind it. The sand proves to be a difficult surface, so I balance it on the rock. Next, I work on the cylindrical branch, stripping away the wood with the edge of the pebble, carving the end into a blunted spike. Inserting the spike into the hole, I twist the branch back and forth, forcing through the ache in my arms and the burning pain in my knees. I smell the smoke though I cannot see it and, taking up the pebble again, I chip into the side of the branch from the edge to meet the burnt hole. Time stretches as I work away, listening to the quiet beyond.

Finally, I feel the loss of resistance as the edge of the pebble reaches the hole. I collapse to the sand, gathering leaves and putting them on top of the rock, balancing the wood over the top of it. Inserting the branch again, I twist and turn it, back and forth, anxious not to let it slip. I know not how long I am there, listening to the friction of the wood. Eventually, I see the faint glow. Victorious, I pull the branch away, fanning air over the coal nestling in the leaves. Gently, I scoop it into the ball of tinder, blowing as I squeeze it.

The ember continues to glow, spreading throughout the tinder. As flame begins to trickle through, I drop it into the pit beneath the cone, on top of dry leaves and bark. The flame catches them easily. I add more tinder, slowly watching the fire grow, before I add my collection of kindling, piece by piece. The fire grasps it greedily, embers sparking before fire engulfs it, spreading wider. I gaze into the bright light as it finally conquers the cone, so dazzling after so much time in semi- to full darkness. I feel the heat. I stretch out my fingers, the glow of dancing flame catching the dull pallor of my skin. It is so papery, I fear if I were to get too close I too would catch alight.

I pull at my damp coat, dragging it from my shoulders, hoping without it the heat can reach my body, to breathe a little life into my tired bones. I lay it on the sand before the fire, sitting back, my eyes drawn into the flames. I close my eyes against the searing light, orange glowing behind my eyelids.

Once more I can hear music. It sounds closer this time than before, when I was on the boat. Opening my eyes, I see her face through the flames.

Who is she to me, that her face permeates my every thought, invades my vision like a spectral vapour, has the moisture stinging in my eyes as I bear witness to her countenance? I feel she was once very important to me and, though my memory does not serve me, I feel the ache of the empty hole left in the space she once occupied in my heart. To whom do I owe the drying salt on my cheeks that came not from the sea that froths beyond the flames, that battered the timbre in which I made my bed and from which I fell into the depths?

I am so sorry for all the pain. You were always my beam of light atop the cliffs on my most treacherous journey.

I let myself weep, instinctively searching pockets for a handkerchief, outside pockets on my suit jacket, an inside pocket.

We were each other's light. I'm sorry my light went out for you.

I pull sheets of paper from my left pocket, sodden from my time in the ocean, the lining of my jacket and my coat powerless to protect them. Envelopes, stuck together so I have to peel them apart. The seals come apart as easily as cotton wool. Folded sheets inside have been glued together by the water. The ink is obscured, in parts washed away, in others run together between the creases in the paper. Only a minor few words remain, not enough to form sentences. I squint to decipher something from it by firelight. Is it addressed Dad? Am I a father, a grandfather even? Could that lend a clue as to how I came to be here?

My hand closes around something solid in my right pocket. I withdraw it, opening my fingers as I look at the small object lying in my palm. An ornament, like those found in a trinket shop in a coastal village. It is a lighthouse, white and red, stood atop a black rock adorned with a white skull and crossbones. The stinging in my eyes registers before the memory that sweeps in like a tidal wave.

The heaviness in my chest grows, an expanding void in my heart that will swallow me up. I feel her so close, yet she has never been further away. I look around at the trees, the sand around my feet and my makeshift fire, to the dark swell of the sea beyond and the dark sky obscured by the fog. I ache to feel her arms around me, to know she is there and I am not alone in a hopeless world. But there is no comfort, not the presence and support of another human being, nor the warmth of a body to ease the chill in my heart.

Instead it is I holding her, her body cold and weak, drained of the blood that colours the water that has gone cold around her, pink rivulets running from her fingers, dripping to the floor as I pull her to me, crying out for her to answer. But her pale face does not form expression, her lips do not form words nor even the smallest smile of reassurance. The ugly wounds on her arms form the only message.

It was a long time afterwards before I could bring myself to read the note she had written for me. A long time after they had all told me there was no villain to blame, no crime to answer. I could not accept that she had acted alone, that this was her choice.

I was so terrified of not being able to love you enough. How can I love you how you deserved when I cannot even love myself?

I could not understand how she truly believed I was better off without her. She was my world. I worshipped her. Beside the fire, I let my tears fall, sobs wracking my entire body. The years went by, each one marled with sorrow, grief still captive over my soul.

I see that day again now, so long ago, when we danced and laughed and made our vows. Yet death could not part us in my heart. Without her, I am a sinking ship, wounded by the treacherous rocks that snared me without her light to guide me.

When someone dies, it feels as if your life has stopped too. We expect the world around us to stop, but it keeps on turning, going on as if nothing significant has happened. How dare it, behaving as if it hadn't shattered today. It is so unfair, so criminal its indifference. I wanted to tear it down, to make it all stop, to make everyone see. We lost someone today. Someone good, someone loved, someone worth crushing the world for, if even for a moment. That would be only just.

How can it all go on, without her in it? I felt so cruel, being alive when she was not. Time goes by, each new day feeling like a betrayal.

There is movement beyond the fire. Is it her? Is this why I am here? How long did I search for a way to find her? Have I finally succeeded? I am on my feet, moving swiftly around the fire, marching with renewed vigour towards the dark, hulking mass that bookends the beach. Water seeps into my shoes, the tide coming in, but I keep on striding.

Reaching the first rocks, I step over them, my leg plunging into a rock pool left earlier in the day by the retreating tide. I sink into the water to my waist, scrambling for a hold on the rocks at the other side, heaving myself out, surprised at the strength in my fatigued body. But I cannot take the time to dwell on it, reaching up with a wet hand for a slippery hold above me, feet scraping and sliding for stability, clinging to the rough edges, grateful for them as the smooth surfaces are too treacherous. I pull upwards, clambering higher. I reach the peak, curling over it, energy spent. Beyond it, the rocks descend to more sand. Wearily, I begin to climb down, finding this equally strenuous. I lose my footing, plunging forward, my body powerless against the sharp edges and slippery surfaces. I hit the sand, expecting the cracking of breaking bones to follow, but they make no sound.

Lying here, I listen to the waves. I should have stayed by the fire, its safety and warmth. The hours I spent building it, yet I have abandoned it in pursuit of– what? A woman who abandoned me? Is that the question I want answered – *why?* Or do I want absolution for my guilt? The guilt of being left behind. The guilt of continuing to live.

The sand muffles my sobbing, the sea blanketing them, both conspiring to hide my shame. Exhausted, I drag myself forward, forward again on to my knees. Wiping the sand and tears from my face, I look ahead of me, a deeper chill dragging on me than temperature alone.

Moored at the edge of the incoming tide is a rowing boat. Jostled by the waves, the slight and indecisive movement punctuates its abandonment.

My captor is here. With me on this island. For I am sure now that they were my captor, that I had no choice in my journeying with them. They and the boat survived the storm, following me to shore, mooring in the next cove. They have watched me, building my fire, remembering my wife. If they did not mean me ill, why not reveal themselves to me? They have watched me struggle – and watch me still.

I remember the hand reaching for me on the boat. I look up and meet their eyes, where they stand further along the shoreline in the shadow of the cliff, barely visible as the moon pierces the fog with the light it doesn't own. The wind off the sea ruffles their cloak. Their eyes are hollow, devoid of life, skin pulled back so tight I can see the white of their skull through it, black eyes like deep sockets. They are grinning, for I can see their teeth, a wickedness to their smile. What do they want with me?

As if in response, their hand reaches out to me once again, a bony claw. I realise they are pointing, not at me, but beyond me. I dare not drop my gaze from theirs. But they continue to point. I tear my eyes away, risking no more than two seconds, only to see nothing. I expect to turn to find them upon me, their quest and cruel intentions for me within their grasp, a bony claw reaching around my throat.

But they are gone, the wind coming off the sea to circle an empty beach, as it pulls cloud and fog to obscure the moon.

I look around, from the corners of the cove, across the sweeping sand down to the sea. I cannot see where they may have gone, unless they lurk in a shadow cast by the cliff or in a crevice hidden in the rock. I have only one clue. I turn in search of it, seeing nothing in my wild haste, running my hands over the rocks in case my eyes are failing me. I put pressure on them, my frustration building. I fear I am simply falling into their trap, that evil grin looming at me out of the darkness.

Suddenly I am pushing at nothing. I stumble into a void. I feel around in front of me, waving my arms ahead. It is the entrance to a cave. My nostrils flare at its dankness, the stench of seaweed and salt. Hearing the ocean behind me, it is a reminder that this cave will soon fill with water as the tide makes its way up the beach. Am I such a fool, to allow myself to be so easily led into a trap? If it leads nowhere, the cave may become my subaqueous grave.

Yet I strive on, albeit with caution.

Soon, I deduce that light must have found a path to filter its way in. Much like in the mist and amongst the trees, I find myself able to see, though dimly and hardly more than a few feet before me. Perhaps my vision has grown accustomed to the solid blackness of the cave, for it is deep night outside and the moon mostly obscured. I can still hear the sea, its waves echoing, having reached the mouth of the cave.

I am heading upwards, the climb growing steeper, though not as slippery as my earlier climb. I hope I have passed the point to which the water will fully climb. I hear it rushing in behind me, followed by a crushing roar of suction as it retreats. I shudder. If I am wrong, I will be trapped here to drown.

I force myself on, impelled to escape the fury of the beast at my ankles. It has grown relentless. I wish she was here to comfort me; a fleeting thought. But since I've remembered who she is, put an identity to her face, she has abandoned me once again.

My face hits solid rock, agony splitting into my head. My hands move around me, my eyes squint to see but they have lost vision. I am surrounded on all sides. I hit out, but I have ascended into a natural alcove, the end of a channel in the cliff. I could be at its centre, so far from the warmth of my fire now, ready to meet oblivion.

Follow me.

I hear her voice and know that I have always heard her voice. It calls to me always. In the night, when I lie alone, I would close my eyes and hear her, calling. I would call back. But when I turn, she would not be there. I would wake, with the tears still wet in my eyes, from a dream of her. Memories, dreams, fantasy; they all feel the same. In all of them, she is here with me. In life, she is not.

I screw my hands into fists, punching the walls of rock, my brittle skin tearing, blood streaming between my knuckles. I hit out above me, beneath me, the cliff squeezing me. I care not if I lose my footing and slip into the watery cavern of the cliff below me.

I am at journey's end. My strength is almost vanquished. My final strike is upwards and I am prepared for the rebounding fall backwards. I can fight no longer.

But I propel forward. The rock above my head is not solid and finally succumbs to force. Light breaks through, with it wind and moisture. The ocean is roaring, fully awake and alert. With bleeding fingers, I pull my spent body up towards the glimmer of light, my shoulders meeting rock. I push my arm through and feel around the opening, more rock downwards, earth and grass upwards. I have reached the summit, up farther than where I sat earlier. I am confident the ocean cannot reach me here.

My shoulders keep pushing. Pebbles and moss give way above me. The rock shifts as my back presses against it. Something touches my hand as it lies on the grass surface. Perhaps an animal investigating such a strange occurrence. But this something has fingers, resting over mine. They feel cold, like hers when I held her hand when I found her.

You are a good man. I didn't believe I could ever be worthy of you, that I could ever love you as much as you deserved.

It is a deep, animal growl that escapes me, ascending to a scream as I force my body into the gap. A boulder breaks free, falling away from me, and I roar at the sky as I teeter on the edge of the cliff, rising from the crevice below, a cry of raw agony and loss and grief.

I see my fire far below, just before it extinguishes as the ocean rushes to claim it. I see the rapidly vanishing beach and the trees and the rocks, the mighty ocean as it spits and rages at them all.

I reach upwards, digging my fingers into the grass, pulling myself forward inch by inch, using my elbows as leverage as I emerge from the ground and crawl from the cliff edge. I close my eyes and feel the ground against my cheek.

It is a long time before I am able to lift my head and look around. Beyond the ground on which I lie is the ocean and the sky. Is that a bird singing? Perhaps it is her singing. I turn over, my back against the ground. Towering above me is a lighthouse, reaching up toward the sky high above and the moon that hangs there like a vast tapestry. Her lighthouse. Our lighthouse.

I am slow, but I succeed in getting to my feet, staggering, stumbling. Behind the lighthouse, the dawn is coming, a dazzling trickling of light, blooming across the hemisphere. At the foot of the lighthouse is an archway. I narrow my eyes against the light. She is there.

She sees me. A radiant smile fills her face and I cry out as I witness it. I run to her, opening my arms as the joy sweeps into me. She cries out too, full of emotion as I get close. I reach out to touch her face, to wipe the tears from her eyes as I always did, for I have found her again. But I find the archway barred.

"No!" I grip the bars with my bleeding hands. She touches them, crying silently.

You need to let go.

I stare at her, horrified she can ask that of me, my eyes pleading with her.

"I've searched for you for so long. I felt so abandoned when you left, so worthless." I am choking.

Please, you must let go.

"No! I cannot. I spent so many years...aching for you. I promised to follow you. I've kept my promise."

She shakes her head, closing her fingers over mine the way she was unable to the last time I held her hand.

You were trapped by grief, let yourself become imprisoned because of the pain caused by my actions. I'm sorry; I'm so, so sorry. If only you can believe me. Please, for me, let it imprison you no longer. You can be free.

Her eyes are burdened with sorrow. My heart breaks all over again. I feel my face cracking. No longer can I form words. I grew old still searching for her every day.

She turns from me, tears pouring down her beautiful face, the face that has haunted me for most of my life. Those eyes so heavy, so tired, are bursting with the agony that I carried with me to this place. I rattle the bars, but they hold as she walks away. I watch her back, sinking to my knees.

I cry out to the rising sun as the sky bleeds crimson, the moon melting like wax, dripping to the ocean, a sea of blood stretching out without end. I can beg no more to hold her one final time.

Rising, I stagger toward the ocean, closing my eyes and hearing the waves far beneath me. The smell of the tide, reaching up, beckoning to me, the cold breeze reaching to give me a helping hand. I stumble, my feet unsteady. I wonder if this is it, the moment.

I fall.

Earth is beneath me instead of water. I open my eyes. I did not reach the edge, have instead fallen on a mound of earth. I look around me. Freshly dug earth, a hole refilled. Urgently, I dig my hands into it, flinging earth behind me. I keep going, pushing it to the sides as I dig deeper. I know I will find her here, that I can hold her again.

As the sun rises, I sink deeper. When my fingers unearth material, I become more frantic, scraping the earth away from it. I recoil as I wipe away the last of the earth.

A skull grins up at me, the same grin I witnessed on the beach in the darkness, the same pale visage that watched me through the mist as I lay at the stern of the boat. My captor, my tormentor, a long-buried corpse. I feel the black material of the hood around their head. I clear more earth from them. Beneath the cloak, they wear a suit. I look at my arms as they clear more earth, look at my jacket. I feel under my collar to my shirt beneath it, slit down my back. I clear more earth, see their hands resting in their lap. From their bony fingers, I prise a small object – a lighthouse, white and red atop a black rock, adorned with a white skull and crossbones.

Please, you must let go.

She was imploring me to let go of life, of all the pain and misery, the grief and despair.

You need to let go.

I rise slowly, the lighthouse still gripped in my hand. But how do I let go? How do I stop all that noise in my head that is barring me from peace? How do I escape my prison?

I pull myself from my own grave, gazing up to the bleeding sky. I pocket the lighthouse.

Numb, I walk back to the lighthouse and around it. There is a winding path down to the cove, only visible by daylight. I set my foot on the gravel, each step sending a spasm through my body. Reaching the sand, I want to crumble, to succumb, but I cannot let myself. I spent an entire life fighting, I do not know how to give in now; devious fragments conspire to feign bodily function, conning others into believing they function as they always have done, together hiding the truth from those remaining, as we travel in this place that twists the laws of nature to its will. The truth of clarity, yet never the clarity of truth.

The boat is still moored where I found it last night. The ocean spared it from its biblical rage. I push it out on to the water, climbing in, untying the rope attached to its anchor, letting it drop to the water, floating away. The long, single oar is wedged beneath a wooden beam. I pull it free and submerge the end, hitting the sand beneath the waves, pushing off.

The sea is calm. After some time, I set down my oar, fatigue dragging on me. I can go no further. I move to the stern, wanting only to sleep. I sink to the solid timbre, feeling it rough against my bones. Beneath the seat is an old coat, which I shrug around my shoulders. I look up to the sky. It no longer bleeds; the sun is directly over me, making my eyes water. It is warm, comforting. Maybe this is when my quest will end. After all this searching, I have finally found her. My eyes close against the dazzling brightness.

I am amongst the lost ones now. Disjointed, fragmented, like I am only pieces of myself, an unknown quantity no longer wholly me, ground to dust and dispersed like slivers of shattered glass, carried as the breeze carries grains across dunes of sand, far and wide and without their own defined and fixed space, without their own identity. Is it possible that in those pieces are parts of me now irretrievable, like an emotion no longer felt, a memory without recollection, a lesson unlearned? Has the whole of me – my body, my mind, my soul – become so unrecognisable that I am no longer myself; that whatever I feel that I am, is simply not, and I am only a single fragment, drifting in desolation and bewilderment, like that single grain of sand, until it snuffs out like dispelled smoke, as all other fragments have been or will soon follow?

PRISONER

Monday

The book quivered in my hands, light glistening off the snake-skin cover. I stroked the lining, down the spine and around the tight binding. The black page edges were smooth as silk. I splayed my fingers over the skin, pulling open the hardcover, parting the delicate pages, which came apart with a gentle elastic pop where adhesive held them together. I pulled back the first page. There she was, nude, kneeling, legs parted, black pubic hair glistening, alluring. Hands rested on muscular thighs, shoulders back, the curve of her back meeting the bulge of her buttocks. Her breasts were heavy between her upper arms, dark nipples erect. Dark hair flowed down her back, two horns protruding from the top of her head and curling around her skull. Her eyes glowed as red as her mouth; lips parted in knowing seduction. She looked at me, captivating me with that look, with her body.

My fingers traced her face, her breasts, her thighs. I was tense, my breathing shallow. She could hurt me, damage me, but I didn't care. I lifted the book to my face and breathed in the scent. The adhesive was intoxicating. There was another scent beneath it. Carnal. Woman.

Eagerly, I flicked through the pages, my tired eyes battling with this hunger. The small, neat print floated across my vision, my fingers caressing the hardcover edges, enjoying the friction. I could fight desire no longer, knowing the wait was almost over. I turned back to the front page, tracing the edges and curves of her body with my forefinger.

I tucked the book away in the bottom drawer of the cabinet, turning the key and then pocketing it. I crept into the bedroom, undressing and preparing for bed in the en-suite. Kayleigh was still sleeping when I crawled into bed. She woke when I entered her, letting the tension of the day flow from me.

I dreamt of her that night, a bounty of flesh, dark hair, gleaming eyes. I was the serpent and I fed on her, sweet as fruit.

Tuesday

"Don't forget, she starts tomorrow."

I jumped as the words were accompanied by a sharp slap on the desk in front of me. Acting Deputy Governor Chapel was interrupting my break as he finished his shift. I couldn't recall what he was talking about.

"New governor, be here first thing," he explained.

"You seem keen?"

"Aye. Good old Acting Governor *Cock*-son can go back to being plain old Deputy Governor." No doubt, losing his acting deputyship suited Chapel. He'd not earned his nickname Chapel o'Rest among the prisoners for nothing.

"See you tomorrow, then," I said, checking my watch and preparing to head back on to the wing. Evening meal was about to begin. My mind drifted to the supplies I'd stored in the boot of the car. I shivered in anticipation.

I stood in the corner, watching the prisoners queue to be served and take their seats, staring at the clock opposite. Hands drifted with painstaking slowness.

My twelve-hour shift ended at eight o'clock that evening. I gratefully got into my car at quarter past, drove home as quickly as I dared and sat for a moment in the drive. Kayleigh was out for the evening as planned. Her mother had feigned disappointment that I would be working late. I doubted my performance was as worthy of an Oscar.

I quickly emptied the boot and carried my supplies into the house. I still had several hours to wait. My hands trembled as I locked the front door behind me. I checked all the windows, making sure there were no cracks between the curtains. I sat on the sofa, fidgeting; got up and paced the room. I checked my watch, then the clock on the mantelpiece. It was only five minutes past nine.

I showered and returned downstairs. I could wait no longer to begin. Entering the sitting room, I pulled back the large rug that covered the hardwood flooring and rolled it up. I retrieved the book from the cabinet, carefully flicking through the pages to re-read the vital chapter.

With white chalk, I began to sketch lines on the floor, careful to make the lines thick and solid. Approximately two metres along the floor, then veering off at an angle another two metres to form the apex of a triangle. From the bottom corner, I chalked a diagonal line through my first. Two metres along, I changed angle, with a straight line intersecting my first two, then the final line at a diagonal to meet my first corner, sealing my artwork. I went back over each line, inch by inch, checking there were no breaks. Satisfied, I tore open the packets in my bag, mixing a concoction of basil, fennel, dill and blueberries. With this, I formed a circle around my pentagram, bunching the herbs and berries so that again there were no breaks in the shape.

I was shivering with a mix of cold and anticipation. I removed the black candles from the bottom of my bag, placing one at each corner of the pentagram, careful not to scuff the chalk. Blood throbbed in my crotch. I could barely breathe with the excitement, building with each passing moment. I checked my watch. It was now past midnight, the moment drawing closer.

I approached the window and parted the curtains a crack. The street was empty, the parked cars darkened and silent. I could see no stars beyond the streetlights and the new moon was hidden from sight. I tucked the curtains back into position.

I took another shower, turning the temperature down to freezing to slow the burning desire prickling all over my body.

When I checked my watch again it was two o'clock.

I returned to the sitting room, retrieving the final items from my bag – a sewing kit, parchment and a quill. To them I added a box of matches from the kitchen drawer.

Naked, I sat in the centre of the pentagram, legs crossed within its inner pentagon. I felt the heat rising all over my body, coursing to my groin. Swollen with desire. My breathing seemed shallow. I struck a match, leaning forward on hands and knees, lighting each candle, black wax immediately dancing on the corners of the flames as the wicks took the blaze, hungry. As I leant forward, lighting the final flame, I had a vision of her behind me, entering me with a roar. I almost lost control of my tightly wound desire.

Sitting back, buttocks on my feet, I tore open the plastic around the sheets of parchment, setting them on the floor. I removed a needle from the sewing kit. Raising my left forefinger, I pierced the pad, pressing it until blood was running freely, dribbling down to my knuckles. I dipped the quill into the wound, setting pen to parchment.

Great Mistress of the Night, I wrote, *hear my desires and bless me with your presence.* I returned the quill to my fingertip, back and forth, a word at a time.

I have ached for your presence, for your company on long nights when nothing can quench my thirst. Allow me a taste of your power in exchange for the worship of your majesty. Satiate my dark desires and show me the path to true ecstasy, where pleasure and pain unite and you reign from your mighty throne.

I had to open the wound again several times with the needle.

All which I have written are my own words and of my own desires, delivered to you with integrity and a sacrifice of blood. I swear my allegiance. I am as One with the Night.

I signed my name, pressuring the pad of my forefinger with my thumb to seal the wound. By the light of the flickering black candle, I read my words. I checked the time. Five minutes until three o'clock.

I had parked in the junction opposite the prison exit, to avoid the possibility you would notice me still parked in the prison car park an hour after my shift had ended. While I waited, I familiarised myself with your social media accounts, the little I could view. It shouldn't come as a surprise that a prison governor was mindful about security, but I was frustrated I could see little more than a profile picture.

Another half an hour went by before I saw you emerging into the car park via the staff door. You were rummaging in your bag for your keys. I started the engine as you got into your car. A few minutes later, you were leaving, indicating right once past the barrier. I pulled out and indicated left, falling in behind you, space for two cars between us.

You drove fast, breaking the speed limit often. I almost lost you at traffic lights twice; the second time I ran straight through them, earning me several angry horns. I was convinced you would have heard them and spotted me in your rear-view mirror. But you made no indication of having noticed, no change in speed or sudden nervousness. When you pulled up in front of a house and switched off the engine, I drove past without altering my speed, performed a three-point turn in the mouth of the next junction and crawled to a stop further down the street as you unlocked your front door.

I pulled the Bowie knife from the glove compartment, unstrapping it from its sheath, watching it glint in the glow of the streetlights. During my break, I'd visited the Roman Catholic chapel in the east wing (we also have a mosque and a non-denominational chapel) and bathed the knife in the font. The book told me a blade cleansed in holy water was the only way to pierce a demon's hide. I re-sheathed it and got out of the car, tucking it into the back of my trousers. I put on a jacket to cover it.

I crossed the street, shrouded by trees as I approached your house. A short path wound from the small gate at the pavement to the front door. You'd left the porchlight on. I crossed the path and approached the window, careful to keep low. I peered through, could see you sitting at the breakfast bar in the open kitchen at the opposite end of the room. You were eating a microwave meal whilst flicking through the pages of a magazine.

You finished eating and stood up. I shrank down further beneath the window. You flicked the magazine closed and emptied the leftover food into the food waste bin. You washed the plastic container and your cutlery, leaving the cutlery to drain and putting the container in a bin that was presumably for recyclables. You left the room through the door from the kitchen.

I walked around the house, feeling the sweat at the small of my back. At the rear of the house was a conservatory, above which was a fenced veranda. Checking through the darkened windows that I would be unobserved, I climbed on top of the waste bin beside the wall and hoisted myself up over the balcony. I stood still, listening, for a few moments, watching the open window, where the wind had caught hold of a net curtain, which flapped around the edges.

I took a step towards the window, then another. The net curtain blowing aside afforded me a view of the room inside. It was your bedroom. You were standing by the bed, in silhouette before the light flooding through the door of an en-suite bathroom. I moved closer. You unbuttoned your blouse, careful with each button, the cotton slowly parting. Your bra was also white cotton. I held my breath as you pulled your blouse back over your shoulders. You laid it on the bed, hands moving to your trousers. My breath was steaming up the glass and I realised that all it would take was one glance and you would see me.

I stepped back as your trousers slipped down your legs. You took them off and gathered them with your blouse, disappearing into the bathroom. I leaned closer. You were leaning forward in front of a large mirror that appeared to cover an entire wall. I froze; had you seen me? But no; a fingertip glazed each eye and I realised you must be removing contact lenses.

You disappeared from view. I pulled the window open further, planning to take my opportunity to enter, when you walked back into the room and I shrank back. You were braless now, your hands pulling your hair back above your head, tying it with something you took from the dressing table opposite the bed. You left the room again, but I waited, my courage dissipated.

I listened to the flow of water, imagining you soaping your naked body. I listened a few more minutes and pulled the window open fully, leaning inside and looking around. The book hadn't specified where it was best to do it, but the shower seemed as good a place as any other, perhaps less messy. The prisoners often chose the showers as the best location to pose an attack. I imagined the blood running over your skin and felt an unwelcome stirring of excitement.

The shower switched off and I ducked back out. I held my breath, waiting for the smallest sound. You may have heard me. I was wasting too much time. I glanced back through the window. You were back in the room, a towel wrapped around you. You crossed to the wardrobe beside the dressing table, opening the central double doors and selecting your clothes for tomorrow. Satisfied, you returned to the bathroom. I heard a tap running.

My breathing was shallow, frosting the glass. You returned. I briefly saw your hairless, naked body illuminated in the light before you extinguished it, pulling the en-suite door closed afterwards.

You slid beneath the bedcovers in the dark. I sat beneath the window. Without the contrast of the light, I could no longer rely on you being unable to see me looking in at you. I waited, listening to your breathing. After a while, it became slower and settled into a gentle rhythm. I raised my head and looked in. The bedsheets had fallen away beneath your breasts. Your nipples were erect from the cold. I watched your parted lips. I craved to taste you, the sweet taste of your lips, the aftertaste of mint toothpaste, the scent of soap on your nipples, the tangy syrup between your legs.

I pushed myself through the open window, desperate for your body. I leaned inside, imagining the blood splashing over your breasts as I plunged the knife between them. I turned away as I reached behind me to unsheathe the knife in readiness. I glanced back into the room.

You were sitting on the edge of the bed. You stared straight at me, eyes glowing red in the darkness. I was sure you were smiling. You parted your legs, the corner of the bedsheet falling over your thigh. You dared me to risk exploring the shadows between them.

I fell backwards, landing with a thud on the balcony floor. My breathing was heavy. I listened to the silence, waiting, expecting the alarm to be raised or to be attacked at any moment. But neither happened. I crawled on to my knees, jutting my head back up over the windowsill.

You lay on the bed, as if you'd not moved from your original position. The bedsheets were tucked up to your neck. I slumped on the ground, confused. I listened. I waited. But my resolve had fled for the night, so I fled with it, accompanied by the memory of your burning eyes.

Friday

I was successful in avoiding you for the entire day. I'm not entirely sure why or for how long I thought I could continue avoiding my senior manager. Only I didn't see you in that light. I saw you as dangerous, a fusion of terror and erotica. I veered between a desperate longing to taste every inch of you and a creeping, cold fear as I saw your eyes glow out of the darkness.

It was customary for a few of us, when the end of our shifts fell on a Friday evening at a reasonable time, that we would go for after-work drinks. Sometimes the evenings concluded after only one or two, while others stretched through the night and into the morning, the amount of alcohol consumed in a quantity substantial enough to be unable to recall its volume. Tonight was developing into the latter.

I was queuing at the bar when I saw you walk in, the door swinging shut with a crash behind you. You caught the eyes of several men on the other side of the bar as you strode towards a space in the queue in your perfectly-fitted suit, the blouse I'd watched you choose last night visible under your jacket.

I stepped back from the bar as you turned your head in my direction, sinking into the crowd that gratefully pooled around me to step closer to the bar. The music buzzed in my ears. I barged into a couple on my way out the door, the woman pulling her boyfriend away from confronting me.

I leaned against a low wall outside. I heard the door open behind me.

"In a hurry to be somewhere?"

I turned. You were framed in the doorway.

"Just going to move the car."

"I don't think that's the most advisable action." You stepped forward. You were smiling. I struggled to decipher it.

I didn't respond, rooted to the spot as you took another step closer.

"I'm beginning to feel you've been avoiding me."

"Of course not." My answer was too quick. You raised your eyebrows.

"I've had one-to-one conversations with every member of my staff during the course of the week. Every one. Except you. Why is that?"

You were close now, your face inches from mine. Your perfume was rich; black opium. You were shorter than me by a few inches. I looked into your scintillating eyes, which looked up at mine with a raw intensity; watched your lips move. I felt something fizzing between us, electric. Your eyes were entrancing. I couldn't trust you. I couldn't trust myself. Being so close to you was too unpredictable. You drew me like a magnet. I could feel myself teetering on the edge.

I lifted my hand and grabbed your hair, pulling it to tilt your face upwards. Your mouth opened, hungry. I kissed you, hard, your body succumbing to mine.

You were still staring at me. I blinked away the fantasy. You said nothing, your gaze a challenge. I shifted my angle slightly, glancing away momentarily. It was enough to disrupt the electricity between us. The moment passed. I knew I could not have resisted it much longer. You knew it too; your eyes held the satisfaction of power. I knew now what your smile meant.

"Enjoy your evening." You turned to walk away. "And your day off."

I remained where I was, head intoxicated with your scent and my own conflicting thoughts.

Saturday

The pages were like silk as I leafed through them, delicate like the pocket New Testament I'd been given in school years before. Words and images flashed before me, arresting, you shackled to an inverted cross, begging me to whip you until you bled, declaring how the thought of me inside you made you throb. But I forced myself on through the book, seeking a specific passage.

Today had been my day off work and, after our encounter last night, I welcomed Kayleigh's suggestion that it should be Date Night in the hope that this would prove a distraction. Yet you kept creeping into my mind. As Kayleigh talked, I saw your mouth. As her fingers circled the lip of the wine glass and fondled the stem, I saw your hand.

It shouldn't have come as a shock to me:

"Is everything alright?"

"Yes, I'm just tired," I said, a weak excuse even as I heard myself say it. It was too quick an answer. She looked crestfallen.

"Is it me?"

"No, of course not." It may have sounded feeble, but I meant it. I was self-aware enough to know that Kayleigh wasn't the problem.

So, we talked and I was able to push you out of my mind for long enough to concentrate on my marriage. Mundane and monotonous life had got in the way of us taking pleasure in it recently. She understood the pressures of work – as a solicitor, she had many of her own. We agreed to make more of an effort with each other, that we needed to put the spark back into our relationship.

We were kissing by the time we left the restaurant and took a taxi back to the house. I pushed thoughts of you out of my mind as I pushed Kayleigh against the front door. I didn't care about the neighbours, watching from their windows. Lust burned in my mouth. I unzipped my trousers, fumbling with hers, but she stopped me.

My hand trembled with anticipation as I heard the bath taps stop running upstairs. Kayleigh was in the bath; images of her soaping her skin with care floated through my head, while you whispered at me from the pages of the book.

I heard her getting out of the bath. I went upstairs to our bedroom.

Water still glistened in droplets from Kayleigh's body, glinting in the reflection of the candles I had spread around our bedroom. She joined me on the bed, kissing my mouth. I ran my fingers through her hair, pulling a red silk sash over her eyes. She emitted a playful giggle as I tied it tight around the back of her head. I pushed her down on the bed, watching her lying there and unable to see anything but flickering colour through her blindfold, arms and legs spread, inviting my body to invade her.

Blood pounded in my head and groin, thick with alcohol and desire. I pictured you, naked as I watched you from your window. You looked up at me, smiling in knowledge, like you had known I was outside all the time.

Kayleigh moaned softly as she felt the weight of my body on hers. I explored her with a finger, a soft groan rising from the back of her throat. I took both her arms, wrapping another silk sash around her wrists, the bedpost between them.

"Wouldn't want you to start without me," I whispered into her ear. She giggled, pulling against the knots with her wrists. I dove into the bathroom. She'd left the bathwater for me and I quickly washed and dried. I gripped the knife to my waist as I turned back to the bedroom. I wrapped a blindfold around my own eyes, entering the room, aware only of patches of red.

"How long were you watching me?" Kayleigh's voice was husky, rich with erotic tension.

I felt cold fingertips drift up my arm.

"That tickles," she mumbled. I hadn't moved from the doorway. "Ohhh, that's good."

I moved towards the bed, step by careful step. Kayleigh moaned. She was pulling on the restraints; I could hear the friction against the bedpost.

"How do I taste?" Kayleigh gasped.

My breath escaped in short bursts. I was at the edge of the bed now. "Incredible," I murmured back, gripping the knife in my right hand, reaching out with the fingers of my left. I collided with skin, so cold, smooth like the scales of a serpent. Buttocks, a hip bone, a thigh. Fuck, you were beautiful.

My eyelids were squeezed shut behind the blindfold. I saw you smile at me, the flash of your eyes, the shadows between your legs.

I raised the knife high, flexing my fingers around the hilt.

Wet suckling, laboured breathing. Kayleigh emitted a guttural groan.

You smiled again, baring your teeth. So evil. So desirable.

My hand was shaking. I plunged the knife.

Kayleigh cried out, a moan of unreserved pleasure. "Don't stop."

I could take the tension no longer, entering you. It felt like plunging deep into ice. Breathless, shocked, I drove deep, Kayleigh's cries louder as your face thrust into her with every thrust I took into you. The knife dropped from my hand and I heard it

54

slip to the floor. I grasped your hips with both my hands, fury building. I let out a roar. Kayleigh could no longer contain her pleasure, screaming in ecstasy.

I reached up and ripped off my blindfold, looking down at your body between us, curled downward, buttocks in the air, face between Kayleigh's legs. A hooded serpent descended from your hip. Heat pulsed in my head.

But you were no more, a spectre disintegrated to vapour. Only Kayleigh and I were on our bed. I threw myself forward, ripping away the restraints as I thrust deeply inside her. We embraced as I bathed in her heat, flooding her, an eruption full of desperate hunger for salvation, in your name.

Afterwards, we lay on our backs, limbs tangled, barely able to breathe.

"That was incredible," Kayleigh said hoarsely.

It was. You were.

Sunday

"Sorry to disturb you, Governor."

You smiled and gave a slight shake of your head, to say it was not a problem. You pushed your glasses up slightly to the bridge of your nose, indicating the seat opposite you with your other hand. I sat gratefully. You looked different, your hair released from its bun and tied back loosely in a ponytail. Loose strands framed your face. Your eyes seemed gentler today.

"How can I help, Officer Freeman?"

"Jer is fine, please." I tried to discourage use of my surname in work – the nicknames and slurs from the prisoners were too predictable. You smiled knowingly. I returned the smile, awkward, faltering. "I just wanted to talk about the rotas."

"You're unsure about your permanent assignment to A Wing?"

I nodded, unable to stop staring at your face. Your lips moved, each word forming a perfect shape. I thought about a hooded serpent, its tongue pointed and precise. I'd only learnt of the change to rotas reading the email this morning.

"Whilst I appreciate the reasons my predecessor chose the course of action to rotate assignments, not least the understaffing, I don't feel it was with the best interests of the prisoners in mind. Building relationships with staff will greatly improve their chances of rehabilitation."

"Sorry, Governor," I stammered. "You misunderstand; I've no objection to the strategy."

You smiled again. You were leaning back in your chair, casual. I felt distinctly aware of your body beneath your suit.

"You've shown a lot of promise as an officer, Jerome. I've read your file. I've observed you with the prisoners. A Wing will give you the opportunity to excel. I'll give you some personal advice. Don't fuck this up."

I watched your mouth form the word. I wanted to fuck that mouth.

"Maybe you will…"

I realised I'd stopped listening. "Sorry, Governor?"

"I was explaining, maybe you will find the change pulls you out of a rut. I make it my business to understand my staff, Jerome. A Wing may house some of the most challenging prisoners, but it may prove to be most rewarding."

"Thank you, Governor." I rose to leave, your collected poise making me feel as if I was moving with too much haste. I wasn't sure what I should say on leaving, instead saying nothing as I shut the door. You were still watching me as it closed between us. For the first time, I had doubts that you and the entity that lay between my wife and I were one and the same.

I glanced back as I left the outer office beyond your own. You were still watching me through the partition glass.

Monday
"The police are here to see you."

Kristoph Kraken's head turned slowly from where he sat on his narrow bed. His eyes had a hollow quality, his face expressionless.

"To what do I owe the pleasure?" No inflection in his tone, no hint at surprise.

"Your guess is as good as mine."

Kraken was easily our most infamous prisoner. Multiple murderer, sexual deviant, leader of a gang that had taken on an almost cult-like status.

He said nothing further as we left the wing, navigating the corridors on the way to the legal suite in the west wing adjacent to the visiting hall. He held out his hands to allow me to cuff him. An incident several years ago where he attacked a police officer deemed him too dangerous to remain unrestrained during visits.

Chapel greeted me as we entered the suite. He opened the adjoining door and ushered Kraken through. Two police officers were sitting on the opposite side of the table, which was bolted to the floor in the centre of the room. I took up position behind a partition window of reinforced glass, not dissimilar to the one-way mirror found in police interrogation rooms, only the lighting often allowed the glass to remain fully transparent. It allowed for confidential conversations with legal representation and law enforcement, while allowing prison staff to observe, if necessary for safety reasons. Kraken sat in front of the police officers – one plain-clothed, the other in uniform – his back to the partition.

"Late night?" Chapel asked. "Your eyes are like piss-holes in the snow."

It had been a late night. I'd followed you home, sitting outside for hours. When you retired to bed, I'd been unable to summon the courage to climb up to your window again.

"Not sleeping too good at the moment," I explained.

"That wee lassie of yours keeping you up at night." Chapel laughed.

"Something like that." I laughed with him.

"Anyhow, I need to be getting on to the wing. See ya later."

I was alone, watching a silent movie playing out before me. Photographs were slid across the table, the detective pointing at them as he talked. Kraken remained immovable, not even a flinch or a turn of the head. I had no idea if he was responding or simply saying nothing.

The detective continued to talk, becoming more animated.

I thought about you upstairs in your office. Did you think about me? Did you fantasise about me inside you while you went down on my wife? I pictured your body, sketched on to the pages of the book.

More photographs were slid across the table, Kraken showing no reaction. I was curious what they were questioning him about. My finger hovered over the speaker switch. In circumstances when a conversation required monitoring or recording, the equipment was available. A red light would illuminate above the inside of the door leading to the corridor in the interview room, so that its occupants would be aware they were being monitored. It was a risk.

I flicked the switch.

There it was. The tiny movement of Kraken's head, his first physical reaction to anything.

"...mutilated women. Raped. Tortured. Sacrificed. All with your semen inside them. How do you explain that?"

Kraken said nothing.

Sweat was pouring down my forehead, my finger on the button, ready to click off the sound.

"Did your followers set this up?" The detective tapped each of the photographs splayed across the table forcefully. "All these murders."

Slowly, Kraken raised his hands from where they rested on the table, holding them out in front of him, separating them until the handcuffs went rigid. He laughed, loud and wicked.

I snapped off the volume and sank into a chair, trying not to make my actions obvious. What was I playing at?

59

The interview didn't last for much longer. As I entered the room to collect him, Kraken met my eyes.

When we returned to his cell, he sat in the exact position I had found him in this morning. I turned to leave.

"I hope you're enjoying the book."

I turned back to him, pulling the cell door closed slightly.

"She's incredible, don't you think?" Kraken's eyes gleamed, deep from the hollow pools. Yet his face remained without expression.

I wanted to tell him I should have never listened to him when he recommended it and told me how to order a copy. But I said nothing, distracted by images of you.

"Keep reading, Officer Free Man."

Tuesday
"Another, sir?"

I looked at the four empty whisky glasses on the small round table in front of me and shook my head at the passing waiter, realising how stupid it had been to order drinks at the bar and take a seat in the hotel lounge. My first mistake – the first I was aware of, anyway. Though, probably, the decision to come here had been the first.

Following another night's vigil outside your home, I knew I wasn't going to have the courage to climb to your bedroom again. In spite of myself, I was excited by waiting outside your house, imagining you inside, wondering what you were doing, what you were wearing, what you were thinking, after I had watched you go upstairs for the night. But that delicious thought of you, in your own bedroom, a predator on your own territory, had me breaking out in shivers, my hand shaking as I took the knife from the glove compartment. Those thoughts were a solid wall which I couldn't bypass. I required neutral ground.

On an early shift today, I'd logged into my email account early this morning and checked your shared calendar. You were due to speak at a conference today – *Rehabilitating Serial Offenders* – at the Barfield Hotel, complete with dinner and room. When my shift ended, with Kayleigh believing I was taking another double, I changed my clothes and headed for the hotel. You were speaking when I joined the crowd gathered at the back of the conference room. You spoke with passion and knowledge; I wondered if the belief at the core of your rhetoric extended to the likes of Kristoph Kraken.

In my new suit, I blended in with the delegates. I managed to keep my distance and avoid drawing any undue attention. Blending in with several hundred people, I was one of them filing to their rooms. You were, thankfully, among the crowd that took the stairs. I risked getting close enough to be able to see the back of your head through the crowd at each turn of the stairs. When I saw you had gone, I ducked back and through the doors, apologising to several people behind me. I saw you in the corridor ahead. I approached once you'd entered your room. Room 3414. I left the hotel in the torrential rain, sitting in my car.

Dinner was at six o'clock. I watched the restaurant filling up through the brightly lit windows. I felt safe to return at six thirty. I went up to your room, knocked the door, my hand already on the handle of the blade as a precaution. No answer. You had gone down to dinner.

So here I sat in the bar lounge, facing away from the lobby, watching reflections in the glass, keeping my head tilted downwards. People were beginning to leave. I concentrated, waiting, reflections bleeding, dissolving in the rain. I kept checking the time.

You crossed the glass before me. I stood up, buttoning my jacket casually, weaving between seats and tables, trying hard to make my haste look like that of a seasoned businessman, not something born of frantic adrenaline.

The door to the stairs was swinging shut. I crossed to it briskly, pulling out my phone, pretending to read a message. I pushed through the door, checking there was no one around and racing up the first flight. I stopped, listening for your footsteps above me.

Click, click, click. The steps were polished marble, cold and hard underfoot. I checked my back, the knife handle jutting into my spine.

I entered your corridor, seeing another door swinging shut ahead of me. I pushed through it, turning a corner. You were entering your room. I heard the door click closed behind you.

The lights flickered, dimming, cutting out for a few seconds before flickering back to life. Thunder rumbled as I approached your room.

3414. I knocked on the door.

The lights in the corridor flickered out.

I held my breath, my hand clutched around the hilt beneath my suit jacket. I knew you were on the other side of the door, watching the dark through the peephole.

I pulled the knife out and held it at my side, my fist clenched so tight I felt as though my knuckles would split my skin.

The emergency lighting flicked on.

The door opened. You looked at me. There were no questions in your deep blue eyes, in the shadows that played over your face. You knew why I had come.

You held a finger to my lips and shook your head. You stepped back into the room, further into the shadows. Thunder rumbled as I entered, letting the door swing shut behind me. I heard it click. Sweating, I raised the knife, approaching you.

Our bodies bumped in the dark. I felt you, a strong, solid mass, your hand on my arm. My heartbeat filled my ears.

Lightning flashed, illuminating your face, inches from mine. Your eyes flashed with it, hypnotic, enticing.

You kissed my mouth, hands on either side of my face. I could feel your heat, responded to your open mouth. Your kiss was wet with lust. Your hands dropped, inspecting my shoulders, sliding over my chest under my jacket.

You bit my lip, pulling it, sucking it. Our mouths clashed again. I felt your tongue, sucked its tip. You pushed my jacket over my shoulders, forcing my arms down.

You bit my tongue. I winced, tasting blood. The knife slipped from my grasp, falling to the floor. You pushed my jacket off and it, too, fell.

Your hands were all over me, tearing at my shirt. You kissed my neck and chest, inhaling my scent. I could feel your breath against my skin. You bit my nipple.

I grabbed you by the arms and threw you from me. You landed on the bed, laughing. There was something crazed about your laugh. Lightning flashed and I could see you, lying on the bed in your crimson cocktail dress, eyes wide.

I was on top of you, kissing that perfect mouth, your wet lips. Satisfaction rose from deep in your throat as I kissed your neck. I pulled the straps of your dress from your shoulders and down your arms. I felt soft breast releasing against my face, my stubble grazing a nipple. I took it into my mouth.

I peeled the dress from you, my mouth exploring the jut of your ribs, the smooth descent to your naval. Lightning lit the room. In the haze, I was face to face with the tattoo of a hooded serpent, eyes like sapphires, rising from where it lay coiled at your hip, hood spread beside your ribs, ready to strike from beneath your breast.

Your knees were bent. I felt the hem of your dress on your thigh. I slid beneath it, pushing your dress down with my hand. The room lit once more in a flash. Your legs spread further, inviting. I tasted you. My head was spinning. My mouth watered, thirsty for your elixir. Your moaning grew more intense as stubble grazed your wet lips.

You rose before me, tasting yourself on my mouth. I sat back on the bed as you manoeuvred on to my lap, your dress gathered around your waist. You undid my trousers beneath you, your body gyrating over mine, never losing contact, your breasts against my face.

The serpent's eyes gleamed at me in the electric haze, tempting me with your forbidden fruit. I could still taste it on my lips.

You were breathing hard as you raised your hand. You held my knife. Your eyes held mine. It was over. I waited, preparing to feel the cold blade slicing into my flesh.

You turned the knife and held the tip of the blade against your stomach, rising and falling with your sharp breathing. Still, you held my gaze. It would be so easy for me to pull your hand, to plunge the knife deep into you, and this would all be over. I would be free of your malign power.

You smiled. I couldn't do it.

You ran the blade up past your ribs to your breast, a red rivulet tearing open. I licked along the wound as the blood dripped from you, my mouth running between your hard abdomen and the soft flesh of your breasts. Your blood tasted like you.

You sank into my lap, locking tight around me. I was now entirely your prisoner.

Wednesday
I'm waiting.

I read the two words in Kayleigh's text message three times. I checked the time on the message. Three minutes ago. I pressed reply.

Where are you?

My hand shook. Kayleigh knew about you.

It shouldn't have happened. I tasted forbidden fruit and now realised it was rotten.

In the legal room.

Why was she here? Maybe she'd waited for me to be on a break, to confront me.

Are you coming?

I knew I had to.

The thunder had woken me at around three o'clock this morning. You weren't there. You hadn't left a note or even your number to reach you. I'd gone home, hoping Kayleigh would be unaware of the time I crept into the spare room. I hadn't wanted to see her this morning, so had rushed out early.

On my way, I replied.

I hadn't seen you all day.

I brought the blindfold.

What?! Was this a trick? Perhaps it was you, playing mind games. Perhaps you had told Kayleigh.

I collided with Chapel in the doorway.

"You escaping somewhere?" he guffawed. I muttered an apology.

"Hey," he called after me down the corridor. "Your lassie was here with one of the juvies earlier. Told her she could stick around and wait for you to come off shift."

I felt the cold sweat trickle down my back.

"That's against protocol."

"What you worried about?"

I shook my head and ran to the legal suite as quickly as I could. Unlocking gates, locking them again behind me, fumbling with my keys. I was still clutching my phone, another breach of protocol.

Tap three times so I know it's you.

The legal suite was in darkness. I tried the adjoining door, but it was locked. I went to the one-way mirror. Kayleigh was sitting at the table in the interview room. She had tied the blindfold around her eyes, waiting for me. The only light trickled in from the door to the corridor.

I heard three taps. The light stretched as the door opened.

You were here. I could feel you.

I could see Kayleigh's chest rising with sharp breaths.

I felt someone approach me and spun around. You stood before me. You trailed a finger down the side of my face.

I gazed into your demonic eyes. You had us both trapped under your accursed lust.

I turned back to warn Kayleigh.

Kristoph Kraken stood behind her. She was leaning over the table, hands gripping the edges as he pushed her trousers partway down her thighs. He watched me as he entered her, his face cracking into the first expression I'd ever witnessed cross his face, that of wicked glee.

I raised my arms to smash against the glass, but you held me back. Kayleigh cried out in desperate pleasure. She called my name, bracing herself against the table and bucking back against Kraken's thrusts. I felt myself weaken as I witnessed pure ecstasy on Kayleigh's face. Only you had ever given her more pleasure.

I felt your lips beside my ear, whispering my name in mockery as I could do nothing but watch. You had me pinned. Kayleigh couldn't hear me through the sound-proofed partition as I shouted her name.

Kraken pulled her hair. She gasped, almost climaxed.

Kraken circled her neck with his other hand, a flash of silver, and cut her throat.

Blood spattered against the other side of the glass.

I cried out, fought against you, but you held strong, restraining me as I struggled. When I had no strength left, you let me sink to the floor, spent of silent screams and inward cries.

The adjoining door opened. Kraken stepped in.

"Escort Kraken back to his cell, Officer Freeman," you instructed.

I couldn't move.

"Don't worry, we'll protect you." You spoke softly now.

"Protect…me?"

"We witnessed you murdering your wife," Kraken explained.

I stared up at him, completely incredulous.

"Your wife, killed with your knife, at your place of work. My DNA inside her, just like all the other victims. It wouldn't take the police long to work out who you are."

Kraken knelt down next to me.

"How long would the cheating, murdering, scumbag screw last in prison would you say?"

I looked up at you, standing beside us.

"I own you," Kraken said. "I'm not the real prisoner. You are."

You didn't react to his words. Were you as trapped as I was?

"I'll take care of it," you said to him. I knew you meant Kayleigh, lying on the floor in the adjoining room, her throat halved, in a pool of blood.

"Leave it twenty-four hours, then report her missing," Kraken told me. "We'll keep her on ice. Our little secret."

I didn't speak, staring at one, then the other, almost trancelike. Just kept staring. Somewhere I heard the distinct sound of a clock.

I escorted Kraken back to his cell. We didn't speak, navigating the dimmed corridors. From his cell door, I spotted the book lying open on his bunk. He picked it up, snapping it shut, stroking the cover.

"She'll make the lonely nights go more quickly."

I shut the door, listening to the bolts shoot into place as I turned the key. I leaned against the wall, faltering. I walked away from Kraken's cell, footsteps echoing in the deserted wing. I pulled the gate to the corridor shut with a clang.

Images of the dim light glistening off the snakeskin cover of Kraken's book played over in my mind, the spine embossed with the sheen of blood.

THE WANDERER

The night was long and dark, as was the road before me. The night was my friend, my comrade, the best companion with whom to travel. The road was another of my friends; I walked it in long stretches by foot, always at night when it was cool. There were times when a stranger let me sit awhile as they journeyed in their cart and I was always grateful for their kindness. Ofttimes, I was alone.

Dusk fell and I crawled out from beneath the tree under which I had camped during the daylight, sheltering from the hot and heavy sunshine in the shade it cast. Stretching in the twilight, I found that the heat of the day had subsided to a warm night. I packed my meagre belongings into my sack, swinging it on to my back and setting off to the east.

No one else walked the road at night. I enjoyed the solitude. Never have I enjoyed the noise that people make, their desire to give voice to trivialities. Rarely did they make noise over important matters. I have watched men argue and fists fly over a game of darts and the question of fair play; watched those same men turn their backs as a woman was stoned in the street. I used to believe that was shame. Other times I attributed it to cowardice. But it was neither of those things. It was indifference.

Dust kicked up in front of me, shoes scuffed on the roughshod road. Along the way I saw a stray dog and several cats; at times a rat or a squirrel scurried across my path. After quite some time walking, I heard hooves approaching behind me from a distance. They rapidly gained on me.

"Hello, fellow traveller." A man's voice, merry, perhaps with liquor. "To where are you travelling on this fine night?"

I stopped and turned, smiling up at the cart. There were two men sat within it.

"I hope to reach the next village before dawn," I replied, not slowing my pace. The man with the reigns, the one who had spoken, slowed his horse to a trot as he drew level with me, slowing him further to a walk.

"You've no hope of reaching it on foot," the same man said. "You can ride with us the rest of the way." We had all slowed to a stop. I looked from the spokesman to his less talkative companion.

"As long as it causes you no trouble."

"No trouble at all."

"That is most kind."

The mute companion moved as I reached to climb up on to the cart, as if to allow me space. As I was halfway through my climb, something heavy hit me on the back of the head. As I fell forward, the talkative man kicked me in the chest, forcing me backwards. I hit the ground on my back, winded, my head throbbing.

The mute man was beside me, wrestling my sack from where it lay in the dirt, tangled with my arm. I tried to keep a hold of it, but he kicked me twice in the ribs. He tore open the sack, contents spilling to the ground around me as he rifled through it, looking only for what interested him, discarding anything else.

"Get a move on!" the talkative man hissed.

The mute man rummaged one last time and threw the empty bag aside, hoisting himself back on the cart.

"You can't just leave him there. What if he's found straight away?"

The man leapt back down, gave my flailing arm a kick, then grabbed it and dragged me off the side of the road. I tumbled into the ditch, feeling dizzy. With a parting kick for good measure, the mute man ran back to the road. I heard the clattering of hooves and rattling of wheels as the cart sped away.

I reached a hand up to feel the back of my head. It was wet and sticky with blood. I tried to sit up, but this came with a wave of nausea accompanied by excruciating agony in my ribs. I collapsed backwards. I must have lost consciousness for a time, though I'm uncertain for how long that may have been.

When I came around, my head was throbbing. I was disorientated. I may have lain there for some time – it may have taken me a little while to recall what had happened to me – but all I can recall is pulling myself up the embankment and rather shakily standing on what I believed to be the edge of the road. I heard galloping in the distance. As it drew closer, I raised my arm weakly to flag down the driver. His horse saw me, but he did not. Veering to the opposite road edge to avoid a collision, the horse emitted a shrill neigh. Unprepared, the driver was powerless to prevent his cart spinning off course, clipping me where I stood before it came to a halt. I was thrown to the ground as the horse stamped its hooves unhappily.

A man called out and jumped down beside me, but I was already losing consciousness again.

The clicking of hooves was the first sensation to invade my senses, burrowing down into my dark cocoon. Click-clack, click-clack, click-clack. It registered before the pain, a hot wave all across my skull, searing in the back of my brain. I felt my body rocking. The dizziness came when I opened my eyes, only slits at first, fearing the increase in pain that registered when I did so, my brain already too overloaded.

I watched the stars in the sky, pinpricks of light on a dark canvas. The movement of my head against the hard surface on which I lay hurt too much. I tried to lift my head slightly. My neck felt weighed down, leaden.

"*Bonsoir, Monsieur.*" A man's voice, though I could not see its owner. He switched to English. "You were in pretty bad shape in the road back there. I could've killed you."

I jolted up, regretting it instantly.

"*Se detendre, mon fils.*" A hand patted my shoulder as I held my head, my eyes squeezed shut. "I suspect you may have a touch of concussion."

I opened my eyes, seeing the man to my left, tucked up in a coat too big for him, wrapped up around his face.

"I collected your belongings from out of the road, such as they were." I thought to nod, but resisted doing so, wondering where we were going. Perhaps I voiced the thought, as he continued: "I couldn't leave you there. My wife will see to you.

73

Stay with us tonight, and you can be on your way tomorrow."

Thank you was in my thoughts, but my brain again grew foggy, so I may not have said it aloud.

I drifted in and out of consciousness for the remainder of the journey, so cannot say how long it took to reach our destination. The man partly helped, mostly carried, me from his cart into his home.

I was on a mattress of straw when I next became aware, a blanket tucked up to my chin, in a dimly lit room with window shutters open, as I could see the stars. Perhaps then, perhaps some time later, I was vaguely aware of the wound to the back of my head being bathed and dressed.

I was woken in the slow hours of the morning, unaware of by what. The pain in my skull had subsided to a dull throb, my vision no longer blurred by dizziness if I concentrated on a single point. I watched a cloud slowly drift high overhead, as I'd done many times before.

The night was pierced by a baby's cry. I had been drifting back to sleep, now once again roused and sure this was the same sound which I had heard a short time ago. I listened intently for movements in the house or more crying, but heard neither. I slept once more, but fitfully.

The sun shone warm on my skin when I woke, already high in the sky. Now fully able to take in my surroundings, I found I lay on a narrow bed, raised several feet off the floor. A stool stood at the foot of the bed. My dirty, bloody clothes were folded neatly on the seat. Beside me, on the floor, was a chest, constructed of wood. Sitting up, I flexed my toes on the floorboards. I gingerly felt the back of my head. Even through the dressing, it was sore to the touch. I winced, and cradled my head in my other hand, supported by my elbow resting on my knee.

Looking out of the window, I could see the track running alongside the fields. This house was set back from the road. I could see a little wooden humpback bridge across a stream, that would have to be crossed in order to reach the road beyond. Cooking bacon and eggs wafted to my nostrils from downstairs. I could hear the rumble of voices and someone moving around below.

My sack was hooked over the side of the stool. I was cautious as I stood to retrieve it, my body protesting at my movement. Sitting back on the bed, I emptied the contents. No money remained, nor the crystals or jewellery that would have looked as if they'd be of any value. My single change of clothing remained, though these were now also soiled with dust and dirt. Some of my least valuable mementoes collected on my travels remained. It occurred to me that I could hold no secrets from this man and his wife. They had seen all that remained of what I owned in this world and me naked as the day as I was born. I was unaccustomed to such intimacy.

I dressed slowly in my second set of clothes, forgoing the clothes neatly piled for me. With effort, I walked to the door and opened it a little, stopping to listen, unsure if I should venture downstairs into this kind family's life. They were talking about me, in French, but I could loosely follow the trail of the conversation.

"I'm only concerned." A woman's voice, presumably the man's wife.

"I couldn't have left him in the road."

"I'm not questioning your actions. We simply know nothing about him."

"His papers will have been stolen along with anything else of value."

"He could be anyone. A migrant, a criminal…"

"I'm sure that, when he wakes, he will be most accommodating in furnishing us with his history and how he came to be beaten in the road. We're not suspicious, judgemental people, Maria; we are good Christians. The man is injured. It is our duty to assist those in need."

There was a pause and clunking against metal.

"You are right, of course. I'm simply being overwrought."

I could hear bowls being placed and thought it may be the suitable time to make my intervention, while conciliation had been reached. I edged through the door and the corridor tipped on an axis before me. I squeezed my eyes shut and reopened them, the axis spinning back. I steadied myself against the doorframe. A narrow, wooden staircase to my right ascended into shadow. I could smell fresh timber. Behind me was another doorway, at the foot of the stairs. The landing was narrow too, another narrow staircase descending below.

I moved my hand along the stone wall for support, coming upon a third door at the end. This one stood open, on to a small room hardly more than three feet wide, adjacent to the room I had been in. The windows both in this room and at the top of the steps were small, rectangular slivers etched into the sides of the building. They reminded me of the windows of prison cells.

I turned to walk down the stairs, vertigo spinning my vision. The stone steps were steep and I had to balance myself with my hands against either wall as I descended. It had become quiet downstairs; perhaps the couple had heard my approach. The steps entered directly into the kitchen, a small table before me. A prematurely-greying woman stood by the large pot that hung over the fire on the wall beyond the table. A rotund, balding man sat at the table.

"*Bonjour, mon ami.*" I recognised the voice from last night.

"*Bonjour. Merci monsieur.*"

He nodded. "*Comment te sens-tu?*"

I managed a nod, gratefully sinking into the seat he indicated across the table. "*Parlez-vous anglais?*"

"*Oui.* Yes."

I smiled. Deciphering and speaking a foreign tongue took far more energy than I could muster. I felt exhausted.

"You should eat." The woman placed a bowl of bacon and eggs in front of me.

"My wife, Maria," the man said.

"Thank you, *Madame.* You have been most kind." I doubted that bacon was common on the table, so I endeavoured to eat as much as I could from my serving to demonstrate my gratitude.

The man introduced himself as Jean. Between mouthfuls, I explained that I was from England, how my parents had died and I, remaining a bachelor and without worldly possessions, chose the life of adventure.

"Only, until last night, I was still seeking it. Life is much the same no matter where you live it, it seems." I laughed, but their faces told me I had been unable to keep the sadness from my laughter.

"You have encountered some misfortune, *mon cher*," Maria said. She shared a glance with Jean.

"You may stay a while to recover," Jean decided.

"I truly am most grateful," I replied. "But I don't wish to trouble you any further. You have a young baby to care for; you don't need me adding to your burden."

They both stared at me, the silence heavy and bulging, ready to burst.

"Forgive me, I didn't…"

"*Mon ami*, we do not have a baby here, young or otherwise." Jean seemed to be putting great effort into not being brusque.

"*Je suis desole*, but last night I heard–"

"My husband speaks the truth," Maria told me, her composure far more effective. "We don't have a child."

"*Pardonne*." I felt embarrassed by their awkward demeanours, unsure what to say further.

"It does not matter," Jean reassured me. "You had quite a bang to the head. There are probably quite a lot of thoughts and memories getting confused right now."

I agreed wholeheartedly as I finished my eggs.

My offers of assistance both in the house and on the land were refused by Jean and Maria, both my hosts insisting I should take the time to recuperate. I retired to the room in which I'd slept, but the claustrophobia made me restless, so accustomed was I to breathing the air without the smoke and dust and stone, with nothing above my head but the stars and clouds.

I took a walk outside, seeing Jean in the distance on the edge of one of the fields. There were several out-buildings, mostly dilapidated. The house itself was stone-built, three storeys, a chimney at either end. The windows were all narrow and uninviting, wooden shutters secured to the inside of all, currently open to allow in the fresh air. The thatch roof was thick, yet weathered.

I considered the constraints of living in a house, wondering if I would ever be in possession of one. I was unsure I could ever turn back from a life on the open road.

I leaned against a fence post, lights fluttering around me like ethereal butterflies. The baby was troubling me. I had distinctly heard it cry.

Nausea trembled through my body. I struggled to stay upright as my legs lost all strength. I heard a cry once more as a second wave hit me, reaching up like a hand from the grave and pulling me downward. The baby's cries accompanied me into the blackness.

Cracks of light splintered through the grim void. There was a moment before I felt the pain, threatening to disrupt the room that was swaying into focus around me. I recognised the sheet hanging above my head as belonging to the bed in which I'd slept last night, if indeed I'd not lost any time.

A damp cloth was being gently rubbed across my forehead; the touch so gentle it almost wasn't there. I closed my eyes, trying to recall my last thoughts.

"Welcome back, *mon etranger*." A soft voice, barely above a whisper. "You collapsed down by the old barn. You're running a fever. That knock to the head is still troubling you."

I tried to speak, but my mouth and throat were dry, a painful croak escaping my lips.

A cup touched my lips, a hand gently supporting the back of my head as I lifted it to drink. My hand closed around the cup, feeling the smooth skin of another, smaller, hand under my own. The water was a blessed relief. My head sank back to the pillow, resting momentarily on the palm of that other small hand. A narrow opisthenar rested against my forehead, presumably testing for temperature.

A dark braid of hair swung before my eyes. I turned my head to see the stool had been pulled up beside the bed. The owner of the hands was a young woman. Her small face was kind, her eyes a startling grey that immediately enraptures one's attention.

"You should sleep," she said, brushing a loose strand of hair across her forehead.

"I just woke up."

She smiled, an expression which lit her face, breaking the resting pout of her lips. She looked down into her lap, not holding my eyes.

"You shouldn't look away. You have a nice smile."

She giggled. "Thank you, *Monsieur*. You are most kind."

"Call me Matthew."

"I'm very pleased to meet you, Matthew."

"Do you not have a name, *Mademoiselle*?" I was smiling and she blushed, looking away again.

"Sophie," she said, looking back at me. "*Je m'appelle Sophie*."

"Pleased to make your acquaintance, Sophie." I held up my hand. She looked at it quizzically, then grasped it with her small, soft hand, dropping it instantly.

"Now, Matthew, you really should sleep." She stood.

"Thank you," I said. She looked at me, not understanding. "For caring for me."

She smiled that smile again. This time she did not look away. I watched it sparkle in her eyes.

"My pleasure, Matthew. Now sleep."

Sleep I did, though fitfully, the throbbing pain in my head waking me, cold sweats saturating my body. My head felt as if it was on fire. I longed for the touch of Sophie's cool skin on my forehead, a blessed relief. I dreamt of her, of that smile, her eyes dancing before me. But then she was no longer there and I woke once more to a piercing baby's cry.

I was in a state of agitation when Jean visited me the next morning.

"The renegades who attacked me, they had a baby with them. Perhaps there will be a ransom demand or they'll sell the baby into slavery…" I was aware I was raving. Jean looked at me as if I were mad, saying nothing. It occurred to me that he may want me out of his home, but I was determined. "We ought to try to track them down."

I tried to get up, but the pain in my head was too great and I faltered on the edge of the bed.

"You need to rest, *mon fils*," Jean said.

I made to object to his advice, but was too weary. I collapsed back to the bed. He must have sensed my defeat and took pity, as he was wont to do.

"I'll make some enquiries in the village. If they travelled through, someone may have heard something. If they did kidnap a baby, the word will have spread by now, even from neighbouring and distant villages."

I nodded in gratitude, knowing there was little more that could be done.

My fever deteriorated over the coming days. My temperature was manic, soaring to an unbearable high before plunging me into icy shivers. I slept frequently, but restlessly, waking with a cloudy head, my body encased in cold sweats. Sophie was by my side each night, soaking a rag and mopping the perspiration from my forehead and neck.

By day I longed for her to be by my side. Jean and Maria alternated sitting beside me at intervals throughout the day. I was incredibly grateful for their kindness, but also grateful for the times I woke and neither of them were there. I knew from their grave expressions and inability to know what to say that I was raving in my slumber. It was a relief to not see troubled eyes at my bedside.

I dreamt often of my assault, making my sleep more fitful. I became aware that I was shouting, felt a soft touch on my arm. My strained muscles relaxed. I felt another hand stroke my cheek. I opened my eyes. Sophie leaned over me.

"Shhh." It could almost have been the wind. Her fingers continued to stroke my face. I gazed up into the depth of her eyes, the line of her small nose, the rosebud of her mouth, an oval chin. Her cheeks flushed under my scrutiny, but no longer did she look away.

My hand trembled as I pushed aside a stray strand of hair from in front of her eye.

"I need to find that baby," I told her.

"You will." She reached for the damp rag to sponge my forehead. "I'm sure of it."

Her faith in me warmed my heart.

"You have a kind heart, Sophie. Don't let the world take that from you."

By the flicker of the candle's flame, I thought I could detect moisture in her eyes.

"You should sleep. I'll be at your bedside until daybreak." The back of her fingers tested my forehead for its temperature.

"If I were well, we would take a walk beneath the stars." Fatigue was claiming me again, but I didn't miss the sadness in her smile.

"I would gladly walk until my feet bleed, *mon vagabond*."

When several days had passed, my fever eventually began to dissipate. In the early hours of the morning I woke, feeling the cool air on my face and chest, not crippled by sweats or shivers. My heart lifted to see Sophie beside me. She had fallen asleep, her head resting in her folded arms, leaning on the edge of my bed. The cloth with which she'd soothed my forehead lay beside the bowl of water on the small chest at my bedside. The candle still burned.

I reached out and gently brushed her hair out of her face. Her eyes fluttered and opened. For the first time I noticed how long her lashes were. Her lips formed a smile. I stroked her cheek.

"*Mon vagabond retourne*," she whispered. "I didn't think you were going to make it."

I had not been aware I was so gravely ill that there had been question over me surviving.

"I have you to thank."

She smiled shyly.

"You should go back to sleep. You need your strength to keep fighting." She rested a palm on my shoulder. I reached up and clasped her hand in mine.

"I think you are my strength. Stay with me?"

"I will."

"You're exhausted." I moved over to make room on the bed. "Rest with me."

Unsure, she rose from the stool and lay beside me, face to face. I traced the line of her jaw to her chin with a fingertip. She laughed, running her fingers through my beard. I felt as if we could share all our thoughts and secrets there, that I could bare my soul to her. I talked about my life in England, how I could not bear the claustrophobia of home. One day, I walked out and never looked back.

I woke with the morning sun shining through the narrow window. The candle had died while I slept. I was alone.

Jean came to me that day to tell me about his trip to the village. No news of a kidnapping had reached those with whom he spoke, nor had there been a sighting of the band of renegades travelling through, with a baby or otherwise. It played on my fatigued mind for the remainder of the day. I was doubting myself, my assurance as to what I had heard cracking and brittle. I tried hard to grasp for clarity, but it slipped further away. I could not place when I had heard those cries, if I was suffering from an hallucination.

I knew that talking it through with Sophie may help me to piece it together. Resolving to do so this evening, I drifted into a light sleep. But Sophie did not come that evening. I sat by candlelight all night, waiting. I felt strangely saddened, like a bond was severed, yet it occurred to me as I watched the first sliver of dawn that I knew nothing of her.

I enquired as to her not attending to me during the night to Maria, but she looked confused by my question and did not respond.

The days were moulding into one, losing the solid boundaries of night and day and progression from one place to the next. Like lava melting through all it encountered, each day had become fluid, past the monotony of each day being unlike another to the days no longer existing, only a continual stream. I felt ungrounded, as if I were floating along this stream. But this was no delusion of peace and tranquillity; lethargy dragged on me like quicksand, while the notion of the food my body greatly needed turned my stomach. Even water made me want to vomit.

The nights were longer and more painful without Sophie. I found myself yearning for her, for the touch of her hand on my brow and the sight of her wide, smiling eyes. My time trapped in this room was blunted, dimmer, without her. I wanted desperately to be able to leave, but my recovery was stilted and I relapsed a little. I felt a fool for allowing myself to develop such an attachment. For so long, I had been free. Letting myself grow fond of the owner of a pretty face and a kind heart had proved to be my undoing. Now I lay in chains, more trapped by my pining heart than by the walls that surrounded me.

Despite the cold breezing through the window, I was burning up as I was shaken awake and a hand clamped over my mouth. Sophie's wild eyes loomed out of the dark, reflecting the silver glow of the moon. Her gaze softened when she saw my eyes register hers and let her hand slip down my cheek.

"*Je suis desole*. I needed to see you." She was whispering.

I didn't trust my voice to respond as quietly, letting my eyes do the questioning.

"I shouldn't be here." She stood and turned away from me, her face shrouded in shadow as if she had pulled a veil down over her head. It may have been my imagination, but I saw the shimmer of tears on the dusting of freckles on her pale cheeks. Fingers brushed her dark hair from her face.

"Has something happened?" I managed to keep my own voice low, though it sounded to me as if it echoed around the room. She flinched.

"*Mon pere* would be unhappy to find I have visited you."

"Your father?" I was puzzled.

"*Mes parents, Jean et Maria*, they have granted you stay in their home." She talked to the wall, her whispers difficult to hear. She was unable to see my surprise. I had assumed she was no relation to Jean and Maria, for they had not mentioned her and insinuated that they lived alone. Therefore, I

86

believed they had sought her help to alleviate the burden of my care. "You must not tell them of us."

Us? My mind was reeling, attempting to process all she had said. I had believed my growing emotional attachment was mine alone, feeling foolish. "Of course not, but..." I could not truthfully recall if I had mentioned Sophie's name, or referred to her otherwise, during my conversations with Jean or Maria. "...please explain what's been happening. They have been nothing but good, Christian people to me; I cannot imagine they would find issue with their daughter being the caring, compassionate human being they surely raised her to be?"

She turned to face me. I saw that there were indeed tears in her eyes, welling and sparkling. They burst the damns of her eyelids, dripping to her cheeks, splashing in freckles and trickling down the sides of her nose, curving her lips. I watched her lower lip tremble as she spoke.

"You cannot know what I have endured. *Mon pere* forbade me to ever speak to a man, telling me of the evils that possessed their hearts. No man can be trusted. No man is safe to be around."

I reached out and took her dainty hand, her skinny fingers cool under my clammy skin. She laced her fingers through mine and sat on the edge of the bed.

"Tell me everything."

So, she did. She told me how she was born in this house, how fiercely protective her father had been of both her and her mother when she was a child. Her vague memories of her early childhood were tattered remnants of playing on the land outside and becoming aware of the intensity with which her father watched her. But she loved him; he was kind and loving and clearly adored his little girl. But his fears grew worse as she grew older. Girls reached an age where men began to notice them, where they drew attention not just from women and the kindly, trusted parish priest. As the years passed, her time on the land became limited. Soon, she was only required to help her mother inside the house. By the age of thirteen, even cooking and cleaning proved to provide too much interaction with the male world, on the rare occasion a deliveryman or farmhand called upon the family.

"My room in the attic became my permanent home, the four walls my only company. At first, I begged to stand in the sun again, or to lie in the grass beneath the stars. At night I sat and gazed through the narrow crevice in the stone that constitutes a window and dreamed of escape. Animals nested in the thatch ceiling, coming in through the roof to visit me. I had never cried with pleasure at seeing a rat fall on to the canopy of my bed as I did in those early days."

That was her life for almost seven years, with only vermin for company. She told me her story in soft tones, sitting on the edge of the bed, close to me so I could hear. There was little emotion, no burst of hurt or anger. This was simply the story of her life, without another to compare it to.

Silence fell between us and we listened to the sounds of the night. She climbed into the bed beside me and I held her, listening to the stillness surrounding us. The sky went from black to navy and she stirred, sitting up.

"I must go. They will wake soon." She got up from the bed, walking softly on her toes to the door.

I sat up anxiously. "Will I see you again?"

She looked back at me, her eyes so full of sorrow. Then she smiled, eyes now sparkling afresh with tears. "You will."

She reached for the door handle, then changed her mind, moving swiftly and soundlessly back to the bed, leaning close to me. She kissed my cheek. Her lips felt like velvet.

"Thank you," she whispered in my ear.

My heart swelled and lurched as she walked away from me.

"Sophie."

This time she didn't look back.

Sophie visited me when she was able, always under the cover of night, after midnight had passed. On the nights she did not come, I comforted myself knowing that the floorboards creaking above my head were as a result of her movements.

She spoke no more of her imprisonment and I did not broach the subject. Instead we spoke of my travels. She reacted as a child would to my tales, eyes wide and exclamations of awe and wonder escaping her lips. I recounted my exploration of the British mainland, how I left Lancashire for London, but found the city too claustrophobic and riddled with disease. I travelled north again for many weeks, stopping in many places as I went, but never for longer than a few days. Months went by and I found myself at John O'Groats. Looking out to the ocean, I knew I had discovered my destiny – I had the heart of a traveller. I spent many months journeying the coast of Scotland as I headed south again. I explored the ruins of Welsh castles and camped close to those that still stood. Still I aimed south, eventually trudging through the treacherous lanes to Land's End, while a fierce storm threatened to drag me from the cliff edge.

Sophie and I lay close together on the bed, so we could speak quietly without being overheard. She begged to hear more, so I told my tales of travelling Europe over the intervening years. I described the great city of Rome, the magnitude of the Colosseum and the Pantheon. I travelled as far as the Acropolis of Athens, then changed direction. From land to land, each painstaking step tested me, until I stood at the End of the World on the south-western tip of Portugal, gazing over the Atlantic, wondering how the New World looked.

Only weeks ago, I stood before the Notre Dame de Paris. The majesty of holy places was enough to instil in me a deep sense of spiritual peace, one I have never been able to find in a home or possessions or other people. Until this moment. I whispered to Sophie that she was as beautiful as Notre Dame; she was *ma dame*. She laughed and I kissed her lips.

I told her how I hoped to travel further, to explore the ruins of Ancient Mesopotamia and hunt for the Hanging Gardens of Babylon. I told her I'd like to take her with me, but she did not respond. Instead, she looked sad.

"We could see the pyramids of Egypt together," I dreamed.

She simply smiled and let me hold her, but she spoke no more that night.

After many days of sickness, my recovery escalated rapidly over those nights spent in Sophie's company. Falling in love was a remedy with which no drug could compete. Either moonlight or candlelight would colour our whispers in the dark, when hands would stifle exclamations of joy or laughter for fear of being overheard. At times we lay in peaceful silence, at others our mouths met to say what words could not convey.

There were nights when she would not visit me, when either her parents were restless or awake. I listened to the movement on the floorboards above my head, knowing she was there.

I was soon able to breakfast with Jean and Maria as I had on the first morning in their home, always careful not to refer to my knowledge of Sophie. But my nocturnal courting did not sit comfortably with me; it was disrespectful to my hosts, irrespective of their ill treatment of their daughter.

"I imagine you wish to return to life on the road when you are fully recovered?" Jean enquired of me one morning, broth steaming before us.

"I have sorely missed the freedom of the open road," I said.

Sophie had asked me the same question the previous night. She knew I was restless, trapped in a single, small room after so many years of travelling.

"You have so many plans, so much more to see," she whispered in my ear in the dark. I could hear the shape of her lips in her words, see the glow of the moonlight in her eyes.

"Come with me," I begged her. But silence was her only answer, as it always was when we talked of the future. Neither of us had put it into words, but it was in every glance, every goodnight kiss. Ours was a love that could never be.

Yet after Jean's words at breakfast that morning, it occurred to me that there may be a possibility of hope. I thought of nothing else all day, walking the land. My eyes were drawn to the house from each point of the compass. I gazed at the thin slits in the stone beneath the roof and wondered if Sophie watched me from one of them. I formulated a plan and resolved to speak of it with her that night.

But she did not come. The house was restless, Jean and Maria both wandering, inside and out of the building. I could hear the pacing above my head, back and forth across the boards. Sophie was as anxious as I, yet we could not reach each other. I leaned as far out of the window as my shoulders would allow, enjoying the cool air. When I thought that a baby's cry reached me on the night air, I knew I could not spend another night in this house.

"You have both been so incredibly kind and charitable to me," I told Jean and Maria the following morning at breakfast. "You have nursed me back to full health. Without your hospitality I would surely be dead, perhaps still in a ditch at the roadside."

Jean dismissed my gratitude with a wave of his hand.

"There are many who would not have done for me what you have done. They would see me and see a vagrant, a man of no abode, and therefore of no honour or humanity. Thank you for not subscribing to ill judgements. You are good people."

"We humbly try to follow the example of the Lord," Jean said.

"Christ was the best of men. It is people like you who prove His death was not in vain." I paused; the couple were genuinely moved by my words. "He taught forgiveness and love for all men; He taught hope. He taught faith. You believe in Him and I believe in you. That is why I have one final request I wish you to consider."

"Of course, *mon ami*. Anything."

"I ask that you grant me permission to marry your daughter."

Neither spoke, their faces masks.

"I understand you fear for her. The world is a truly frightening prospect. But I have seen it. There is so much beauty, so much life. I promise you, both, that I shall cherish Sophie until the day I die. I shall protect her from the evils you fear and show her the beauty I have seen."

Still no response was forthcoming.

"Maria, you know that good men exist. You found one of them. I am a good man too. I love your daughter."

A tear slid down Maria's cheek. Jean rose slowly from his chair.

"Get out of my house." His voice was like grit.

"Jean, *Monsieur*."

He exploded.

"How dare you! You abuse our hospitality so, you upset my wife, you disrespect me in my own home. Get out. *Immediatement!*" He was shouting, now rounding the table towards me. "*Vous etes un predateur, un dement*." He continued shouting, but I could no longer grasp it.

"*Je vous demande pardon, Monsieur*, I meant no offence. I do not wish to take Sophie from you. For her, I shall give up my life of travels, we–"

"*Monsieur, vous etes fou.*" Jean was screaming, dragging me from the chair. He pushed me in the direction of the door. I could have fought him, but I felt I had no right to do so. He manhandled me quite unnecessarily out into the yard.

"*Desole, Monsieur*," I said. "Please consider what I have said."

"*Monsieur*, do you think my wife and I to be stupid? Do you take us for fools? All of your rambling and crying out in the night, muttering the name of Sophie and hearing babies crying. Do you think we are blind to this? You are mad, *Monsieur*. We have helped you back to health, but we can no longer have you in our house."

"Please," I began again. "I have done nothing but honour you and your daughter."

"I do not have a daughter, *Monsieur*." All the rage had seeped away from him now, like he had deflated. "Believe my words, if you know what to be good for you. Now, please leave us in peace. *Bonne chance*." He turned away from me and shut the door. I stared after him, dumbfounded.

An owl tooted and flew into the moon, shrinking to a speck. A wolf howled in the distance, having come down from the mountains. I was still up to my calves in the sludge of the riverbank, leaning against the rafters beneath the humpback bridge, watching the lights in the stone house I had departed this morning.

Dusk fell, cold moving up the river on the mist as the veil descended. I waded out of the mud and stole towards the house. A curl of smoke was still visible above the chimney against the dark navy sky. I stooped low and kept close to the wall when I reached the building, craning my neck to glance through the window and around the interior. The kitchen was deserted, the only light the fire left smouldering in the coals beneath the large cooking pot in the chimney alcove.

I climbed in through the window, my feet hitting the dirt floor. I moved quickly to the staircase, listening before ascending. I ducked into the narrow room beside the room in which I'd stayed. The murmur of voices carried from the floor above. Jean and Maria were with Sophie. I thought this may be my opportunity to confront them, pull away the mask of lies.

I could smell the timber from which the stairs had been cut and sanded as I approached, a staircase Jean must have spent hours in the barn creating; sawing and planing each panel to build a secure stairway into the attic, where their daughter's room was to be. Shadows cast by candlelight moved on the wall as I reached a bend. I crouched down so as not to be seen through the open doorway, the murmuring forming into words.

Jean stood with his back to the stairs, blocking most of the low, narrow doorway, architrave also constructed from wood, an archway built into the top of the staircase.

"We love you very much, Sophie," Maria was whispering in French. "My little angel. *Ma petite ange.*"

Jean moved out of the doorway, allowing me a view of the room. Maria was sitting on the bed in front of the doorway. I recoiled, almost stumbling down the stairs. In her arms, she held a baby. She continued to whisper to her, telling her to sleep now.

Unnerved, I backed down the stairs, only by the grace of God not making a sound to alert them to my presence. Standing in the landing, I looked up to the ceiling, struggling to make sense of what I had seen and heard. I backed across the landing, reaching the top of the steps. I glanced to my left.

She was there, facing the open shutters of the narrow window. I entered the room, approaching her.

"Sophie?"

She turned to me. Her eyes were glistening.

"Who are you?" I asked.

Her face cracked as if her heart were breaking.

"You know who I am."

I gazed into her wide eyes. Such beautiful, hypnotic eyes.

"Many years from now, I shall finally make my escape and travel by foot on the road as you have for much of your life. But it transpires that my father was right to fear for my safety out in the world, to fear the harm men would do to me. This is a land of lawlessness. A band of renegades will offer to help me, but their desire will only be to help themselves. I was in so much pain. Yet it felt almost like a release. It matched the pain I felt inside. Finally, it will be over."

I turned away, my hand curled into a fist colliding with the stone wall. This could not be. I could not be hearing these words. But the smell of new timber told me the truth.

"I was lost. I had to come home. So here I am, full circle. At the very beginning."

I squeezed my eyes shut. Blood trickled between my knuckles. The Sophie I knew was dead. But not yet. She wasn't even the Sophie I knew yet. I realised she never would be, not in this life.

Yet I was now gripped by a greater revulsion: that my actions, here today, will lead to Jean and Maria's intense paranoia and the suffering that Sophie will endure throughout her life. Actions that I could not put right; instead I have to turn my back on her and walk away.

I felt her steadying me as my body threatened to crumble. I turned and met her eyes. Beautiful voids. Fingertips gently closed my eyes. She whispered in my ear. Tears breached my eyelids and splashed down my cheeks. Her lips found mine, an electric current stopping time. For a moment, I basked in eternity.

When I opened my eyes, she was gone.

The old cart I had commandeered from the stable along with a young mule rocked back and forth over the uneven terrain. For moments, I felt Sophie's hand in mine, her head resting on my shoulder. Fleeting moments, over as soon as they occurred. I knew that they would slip further away from me. My heart ached harder.

Like a husk in the corner of the room in which she'd left me, I escaped Jean and Maria's attention. When they had been sleeping for several hours, I crept up the stairs Jean had recently installed to

Sophie's room and watched her sleep for a while. Barely months old.

"Please forgive me," I prayed.

Her words would never leave me, whispered to me in the dark:

"I can hear your pain, calling to me across the chasm of a dark void, cutting like shattered glass on skin. I know I cannot heal it, cannot dress the wounds or anaesthetise to numb the agony. I know you cannot feel the comfort of my arms around you and do not even know when I am there. But know that I always am. In the darkest hours of the night, you will find me there. So, if, even for a moment, you feel the touch of my hand or hear the sound of my voice, believe in it and hold on to it, steady and true. I have not left you. I live forever in your heart."

I watched the road wind away in the distance before me, as I tapped the bundle by my side. I felt peace, at one with the road, a wanderer – Sophie's vagabond.

A wheel jolted over a rock, the cart shaking, the mule losing confidence in its precarious load for a moment. As we continued on our journey, I held the bundle a little tighter as it stirred, a baby's cry piercing the night.

I KILLED DORIAN

Ed lay on the bedcovers, quietly dozing, a contented smile on his face. It had been good sex – no, great sex, probably the best he'd had with a stranger yet. It was the thrill of the unknown, the excitement of a new body to explore, that gave him his pleasures with a stranger. But a stranger did not know what he liked, the best spots to touch, how his body worked. If he was lucky, they'd make a good guess, while the more conscientious lover would put effort into working it out. Unfortunately, in his experience, the majority of strangers were in it for themselves. But he had hit the jackpot on his lucky dip tonight.

He had been surprised by how much he enjoyed the conversation, too. #613 had insisted on dinner, which they'd decided to consist of a takeout and a bottle of wine. They'd got on really well, much laughter preceding the moment when they found themselves kissing, shortly followed by the sex for which they had arranged to meet. He supposed it may have been due to the weeks they'd spent messaging, known only to each other as #972 and #613, but it felt as if they knew each other. He had never 'made love' to a stranger before. At that thought, he scolded himself with a frown.

He listened to the humming drifting through the wall, masked by the thundering of the shower. The flow of water abruptly switched off; he heard the shower door being pulled back, his lover exiting the shower cubicle. In the silence, he imagined him wiping the condensation from the mirror with the flat of his palm, combing his dark hair back from his face, pummelling himself dry with a towel.

The silence continued. Ed wondered if he had now become bashful, so different to the man he was when desire coursed through his body. Rising from the bed, Ed shrugged on one of the white fluffy robes provided by the hotel and passed the easy chair beside the wall, rounding the corner and walking the short distance to the bathroom door. He knocked.

"You okay in there?"

No answer. He knocked again.

"Everything okay?" He pushed open the door, greeted by a cloud of steam.

Stepping in, he slipped on the treacherous tiles, hitting his knee hard on the floor and cursing. Looking towards the shower, he cried out in horror. Slumped in the cubicle, his head at an unnatural angle, was the man whose real name he did not know. Ed got to his feet quickly, rushing forward. The mirror, as he had imagined, was steamed up, but he registered movement behind him in the foggy reflection.

Turning sharply, he slipped backwards on to the floor. His eyes widened in alarm. He saw a man, rising from the bath, clad in full black, a latex mask tight over his head, zips for mouth and eyes.

The intruder stepped from the bath, a gloved hand reaching for Ed.

Ed scrabbled backwards, even as the intruder's other hand raised into his line of vision, the blade of an ice pick reflecting the light as it plunged towards him. He pushed himself away and to his feet, balancing himself against the washbasin. But the intruder was too quick, already behind him, grabbing hold of his head and barrelling him forwards into the glass, the mirror splintering outwards from the point of impact.

The intruder raised the ice pick, swinging his arm around Ed's head, and plunged it through his eyeball.

Detective Fiennes grimaced. There was no sugar in the coffee. He tossed the cup into the nearest trash can, further irritation added to his day. This wasn't his case; he shouldn't need to be here. He'd been summoned to the hotel when Fletcher, the detective assigned, had called to tell him there was something he needed to see. He didn't recall Fletch's promotion to Lieutenant. Nevertheless, here he was, despite having his own caseload to keep him busy.

There was a queue for the elevator, so he took the stairs to the first floor and made his way down the long, narrow corridor to Room 119. Detective Fletcher greeted him in the doorway, his pot belly protruding into the corridor.

"You took long enough."

"Come off it, Fletch, you know how it is. What's the score here and what you need me for?" Fiennes pulled on an oversuit and shoes covers, finished with nitrile gloves.

"Two dead, both male, Caucasian, 25-35, no IDs." Fletch gestured to the bathroom door on the left as he stepped back into the hotel room. Fiennes walked ahead of him to the bathroom doorway. The two victims were both naked, propped against the

101

bath in a sitting position, backs to the panel. Both had full-hooded latex masks over their heads, black with no sockets for eyes, nose or mouth. Blood smeared the tiled floor.

"Suffocated?"

"No. John Doe A appears to have a broken neck on preliminary examination. John Doe B was likely stabbed judging by the amount of blood, but we've not had a look at the wound yet."

The medical examiner was taking photographs in situ, preparing to transport the bodies now the scene had been processed by the CSIs.

"And the killer?" Fiennes asked.

"Not a trace yet. We're checking the hotel records as we speak, see if we get a lead on the killer or victims' IDs. But I'm not sure how much effort he'll have made to cover his tracks. In fact, he's even told us his name. Take a look." He gestured behind the door and Fiennes walked further into the room. Opposite the bodies was the bathroom mirror. A message had been smudged in blood:

A little gift, Det. Fiennes, for old time's sake.
Yours, Dorian.

"You know this Dorian? The name mean anything to you?"

Fiennes re-read the message, already shaking his head. "Means nothing to me."

"Well, he seems to know you."

Fiennes said nothing.

"Something you've not been telling us?" one of the CSIs chipped in. He held up his camera and the flash blinded Fiennes, who raised his hand too late.

102

Fletch laughed. Fiennes wasn't laughing. He glared at Fletch.

"Fletch, I got something." It was Detective Lawrence, new to the job. Fiennes and Fletch went out into the corridor to meet her. She grinned at Fiennes, which softened his irritation somewhat. Petite, blond, and the most dedicated detective in the precinct. Though he doubted she'd appreciate the list in that order.

"Hotel was booked in the name of Edward Sheerer, double en-suite, no second guest's name provided. Checked in at 1800 hours, took both key cards, booked a reservation for the restaurant for 2000 hours, he and his guest never showed for dinner. However, concierge remembers a takeout being delivered for Room 119 around twenty minutes later, one male came to collect at the front desk. He's unsure if it was the same guy who checked in, but they are currently transferring the security footage to USB drive for us."

Fletch slapped Lawrence's back. "Good work, Law, we might just have him. The vics got more than they bargained for from this little gang bang."

Fiennes wasn't so convinced. "How does he know my name?"

"Well, I doubt it'll matter. Won't take us long to catch this one. But until then, I suggest you watch your back." Fletch grinned, encouraged by roars of laughter from some of the crime scene investigators. Fiennes grimaced, getting a weak smile from Lawrence. It was going to be a long day.

I pushed harder against the floor even as my arms screamed at me in agony. All the muscles in my arms and torso felt so tight they could snap. I ended my ninety-minute workout with weights and push-ups, now in the final stretch as I waited for the shower to heat to optimum temperature.

Ninety-five, ninety-six...

Blood pounded in my head; at each count I could see the bursting eyeball reflected in the mirror.

Ninety-nine, one-hundred.

I let my knees take my weight, at first leaning on my palms, then arching my back as my chest heaved. My biceps bulged. I flexed the tight muscles in my neck and shoulders as I stood. The muscles in my abdomen rippled as I took in deep breaths, stepping through the steam into the shower.

Fiennes was home far later than he had intended. He could hear the TV on in the living room of the apartment as he headed straight for the kitchen, grabbing a beer from the fridge.

They'd not made much progress. As it turned out, Edward Sheerer was one of the victims, easily identified when the gimp mask was removed and his bloody eye cleaned up. They still had no ID on the second victim, with no record in Sheerer's life that he had known him. Fiennes got the impression that his father was more shocked by his son's sexual preferences than his murder. After a thorough search of the hotel suite, neither mans' wallets or cell phones were found. They'd drawn a blank on running the second man's prints – he wasn't previously known to them.

He'd also drawn a blank on reviewing his past cases. He started with the unsolved, moved to those where they'd failed to secure a conviction, then those where he knew the perp would now be out. Nothing: no comparisons, similarities, or anyone who struck him as having held a particularly strong grudge singularly for him.

He finished the beer in a long gulp and took another, walking through to the living room. "Sorry, Sim, it's been a long day."

Simone was lying on the couch, the remainder of a bottle of wine on the table beside her. She sat up, undecided whether to be annoyed or understanding. His face decided for her as he sank into the couch where her head had been resting.

"Tough day?"

"Something like that," was all he managed as a reply. Her robe had fallen open and she caught him looking.

"Now?"

He took a swig of his beer and nodded. She straddled his legs, pulling at his belt. Their kiss was drunk. Fiennes tried to relax as she moved in his lap. It was no good. He couldn't feel anything.

He manoeuvred her into lying on her back, he on top of her and between her legs. But after a few attempts, he knew it just wasn't working. He sat up, frustrated.

"It doesn't matter," Simone lied.

Fiennes said nothing. What sort of man couldn't have sex with his girlfriend? He knew she thought he didn't find her attractive anymore, that the problem was him not wanting it.

"I'm just going to take a shower," he said, getting up from the couch. Simone didn't stop him, just pulled her robe back around herself.

Fiennes switched on the flow of water, slowly getting undressed. He leaned heavily against the wall as the room filled with steam. He sighed, searching for today's excuse. Opening his eyes, he turned to the shower, the mirror above the basin catching his eye. Revealed by the steam, previously wiped in the condensation in a childish scrawl, were thirteen letters:

I KILLED DORIAN

Carmen woke quietly, lying on her front with the luxurious quilt over her up to her shoulders, her face buried between two pillows. She must have dozed off while basking in the warm afterglow of their satisfying sex. Deeply satisfying sex. She couldn't have been asleep for long – he had said he was taking a shower and would then go down to the lobby to await their takeout delivery.

She didn't want to move, wondered if he'd be happy to stay the night. If she was honest with herself, she hoped for a repeat performance. In fact, it might be nice to be sleeping with the same guy for a while. There had been instant chemistry, probably due to the number of weeks they'd been messaging.

She sat up, switching on the overhead lamp with the switch at the bedside. She searched for her cell phone, but couldn't find it. Must have left it in her bag; she couldn't remember doing anything when she came to the room other than taking her clothes off. She stood, guessing he was in the bathroom. Only then did she think – she didn't know his name.

"Hey," she called as she padded naked to the bathroom. "Did the takeout come?"

She pushed open the door, greeted by a cloud of steam. She flicked the light switch, but that didn't seem to improve the visibility much. The shower was still on. She grinned wickedly to herself, switching off the light again and walking to the tub, covered with a shower curtain.

Pulling it back slightly, she quickly climbed into the tub on to her knees, expecting a cry of surprise of which she would soon change the tone. Only, she found herself alone in the tub, water spitting in her face, already pooling at her knees. She felt entirely foolish as she switched off the water.

"Wanker," she muttered as she yanked back the shower curtain. There she was hoping #613 would become a regular fixture, while all he wanted was a quick lay with #844. And he'd not even left her the takeout!

Wiping her legs with a towel, she decided she would see if anyone was up for joining her for the rest of the evening on her deserter's credit card. Suddenly it occurred to her that her own cards and phone may have left with #613. She rushed back to the bedside, clamping a scream back into her throat with her hand.

Her evening lover lay sprawled on the bed in the dark, naked, like he'd not left the bed at all. His eyes stared dully at her, his head at an awkward angle.

Stirring herself into action, she turned and collided with a solid mass, stumbling backwards. The black-clad intruder moved, latex rippling. No face, only a black hole in the darkness. Nonsensically, Carmen thought how he must have extinguished the lights.

The intruder raised a hand and Carmen finally let out a scream as the blade plunged towards her face.

"You look like shit."

Fiennes could do little more than grimace. He was late and had managed little sleep. What he had managed had been plagued by the sound of water dripping, running steadily from writing in the condensation on a mirror.

A ripple of laughter broke out around the room. Nonplussed, Fiennes looked around at the group of detectives; then his photograph on the board caught his eye. He looked ridiculous in his Tyvek suit, captured in a moment he wasn't expecting like a paparazzi victim.

"Seriously…"

"You show up late and immediately you're complaining," Fletch said.

Fiennes swallowed his retort congratulating Fletch on his promotion. Instead he replied: "I've been thinking…about Dorian. I…"

"There's been another one." Detective Lawrence had burst into the room.

What followed was a frenzy of activity. Fiennes accompanied Fletch to the crime scene, another hotel room, two more victims. This time they were lying on the bed, side by side, masked, but otherwise naked. Cell phones and IDs had been removed, though the room was booked under the name of John Masden, with a credit card linked to the booking. Whether this was a false name or not, they would be able to track him down through the credit card company, but they had no doubt he would prove to be their male victim, as Edward Sheerer had proved to be one of their victims the first time.

"How is he arranging all this?" Fletch exclaimed, exasperated. They were back at the precinct, studying the crime scene photographs on the monitor. Lawrence had just called from the morgue – one more difference this time; the Jane Doe was missing both eyes.

"Is it just random?" Fletch continued. "Just picking random couples? How does he get through locked doors? Taking on two people is brave."

"Maybe he appears to them like an apparition."

"What, like a ghost? Ghosts don't break people's necks and gouge their eyes out." Fletch slammed the desk with his hand. "What's with you?"

There had been another message for Fiennes at the crime scene, this time on the mirror opposite the bed.

Still no closer, Det. Fiennes. Catch me if you can!
Love, Dorian x

"I know who Dorian is."

"What?" Fletch spluttered.

"I remembered last night. The only Dorian I've ever known. He was in high school with me, three grades below. His sister was in the grade below me, I think. Anyhow, the only reason I remember him – he was being bullied, tormented by older kids. My age, his sister's age. One night it all just got too much for him – he hanged himself."

Fletch was silent for a moment.

"What was this kid's surname?"

"I don't remember. All I could remember was Dorian. They used to call him Dora. Fat little Dora who emptied the store-r."

"Well, one thing's for sure. Little Dorian hasn't come back from the dead. And why the fixation with you? Did you bully the kid?"

"No." Fiennes shook his head. "I wasn't even aware of him until he committed suicide."

"Well, it's a possible lead. Let's track down his family, find out what happened to them."

Fiennes' cell phone started to ring. He glanced at the caller ID, horrified.

Dorian calling...

"Hello?"

"Babe, what is taking so long? I've been waiting here for half an hour."

Fiennes checked the caller ID again and groaned, more from relief than displeasure.

"Sorry, there's been another one, another two. I didn't realise what time it was."

"You never do." Simone had long ago mastered sarcasm. "I might see you later then."

Silence met Fiennes' attempts at protest. He looked out the window, convinced for a split second he could see a rope, tightening as if a weight had just dropped on the end of it.

Simone cast her cell phone to the table, regretting her words. She was aware she was rarely understanding of Fiennes' feelings.

She stared at her phone where it now lay on the centre of the table at the fast food restaurant where they'd arranged, and failed, to meet for lunch. She sighed, thinking how she ought to be used to this by

110

now. Long before their marriage, this was how he had been, rarely attentive, never romantic, barely considerate. She shouldn't still feel disappointment now. Not so many years later. Hell, she'd had a better deal than some of his high school ex-girlfriends.

She picked up her phone, flicking through the apps, back and forth on the screen. Just one more time? She fidgeted with her clothes, looked around the restaurant, back to her screen. She wasn't sure she could cope with the guilt again, her heart sinking into the pit of her stomach every time he came home, wondering if today would be the day he knew. But there was that one guy she couldn't quite get out of her head. #613.

She was only half aware of the door opening behind her and someone entering just as a group were getting up to leave. She snapped out of her thoughts as they lurched into her chair in an attempt to avoid the inconsiderate crowd.

She turned sharply, hearing the heartfelt apology only a split second before recognition registered on both sides.

"Oh my God – Dan? I haven't seen you since, well, it must have been high school!" Simone stood, embracing her equally enthusiastic old friend to her. "Funnily enough, I was just thinking about the high school days."

Dan held her at arm's length, smiling in response, apologising again.

"Nonsense," Simone replied, gazing at the intense blue eyes she remembered so well.

"Can I get you a coffee? You got time?"

Simone nodded. "My husband just cancelled our lunch. I'm all yours."

"Husband? We do have some catching up to do." Dan went to get the drinks as Simone sat down again. A catch-up with Dan would do her good, she thought – they did have a lot of catching up to do. Perhaps, in particular, about one thing. She had told herself the last time that it would be the last time. But another once wouldn't make much difference, would it?

I was determined not to give in to the strain, the barbell feeling as if it had gained weight each time I brought it to my chest and pushed back up again. It was almost time and I was ready.

The second killings had proved as seamless as the first. But tonight would take more finesse.

Ninety-eight, ninety-nine…

One more push and I let the bar rest.

I was ready and they were waiting for me.

Jenna gratefully let the water wash over her body. The hotel suite was luxurious, the takeout had been delicious, and the sex was raw and sensual. #613 was a catch, even if this, strictly speaking, wasn't a date.

She soaped her body, rinsing it off with the showerhead; pummelled herself dry with the thickest, softest towel she'd ever used, and took advantage of the provided scrub and exfoliator for her face; standing in front of the wide mirror behind the double basin she had to wipe free of condensation. They could have showered together. But perhaps that would be too intimate.

Leaving the bathroom, she entered the dark bedroom, seeing the shapely form of #613 under the luxury quilt. She smiled, pulling off her towel.

"You going to kick me out now? Only, I'm not really dressed for it."

She was disappointed her statement didn't result in the immediate inspection of her lack of garments and one of the quick-fire smart responses she'd already grown accustomed to this evening. In fact, she received no response. Well, she certainly hadn't made much of an impression. Feeling rather foolish standing in the middle of the room, naked with a damp towel at her feet, she went to the closet opposite the bathroom door to fetch a robe, swallowing crushing disappointment. Back to square one after one night!

She shrieked as a human form lunged at her out of the closet. It erupted to a full-bodied scream as the person slumped at her feet. Her lover, head at a bizarre sideways angle, as if glancing over her shoulder with the bloody sockets where her eyes had been.

Behind her, the bedcovers shifted and the intruder sat up in the bed, turning their gaze in her direction as she turned to them. The face was featureless and blank, not a face at all.

Jenna raced for the door, only feet away from her. Yanking on the handle, it caught on the latch, which she wasted valuable seconds fumbling with before slamming the door into place and pulling it free.

The intruder was on her, her body crashing into the door under the force of enormous strength. She pounded her fists against the wood, kicking out as she was pulled around, her back slammed against the door, taking the wind out of her

There was a flash of metal before her and an excruciating pain in her left eye. She scratched and clawed in front of her, frantic; she kicked, she punched, she bit; her entire body in a frenzy. In seconds it dawned on her that one of her defences had granted her temporary release. She pulled on the door handle, almost falling into the corridor, a haven of bright light only one eye could see.

She ran as fast as she could, screaming out for help as loud as she could manage, feeling the intruder in pursuit close behind her. She tripped and fell, crying out in one last, desperate call for help.

A hand closed over her shoulder from above.

Fiennes was home late for the second night running, after another long and fruitless day. The second set of victims had not moved the investigation forward – in fact, they felt they had stalled. No forensic evidence, no eyewitness accounts, no leads arising from the lives of Edward Sheerer and John Masden and no link uncovered between them. Equally, there appeared to be no links between either of them and their respective John Doe and Jane Doe, with no one matching their descriptions known to their family, friends or work colleagues. Missing persons reports filed in the last forty-eight hours also did not match either of their descriptions.

Unable to find a lead via the victims, this led them, inevitably of course, to examining the killer. What was his motivation? There was no obvious sexual element to the crimes; you could assume voyeurism, but that also didn't seem to be a straightforward solution. For their first pair of victims to be a male homosexual couple, and their second pair to be a heterosexual couple, was unusual. Each turn implied a greater complexity to the orchestration of the crimes – there could be nothing random about the selection. Was the killer linked to the two unidentified victims, thus explaining the attempts to conceal identity? If that was the case, how would the killer know that their partners would book and pay for the hotel rooms? There must be a trail; Fiennes believed they would find it on the victims' cell phones, all four of which had been removed from the scenes. They had requested phone records and analysis of social media accounts of the two known victims – perhaps this may lead them to the identities of the unknown victims and subsequently to their murderer.

Fiennes opened the bathroom door, looking at the mirror. There had been much theorising as to how 'Dorian' was gaining access to the locked rooms. Did one, or both, of the victims in each room let him in? Had he a trick to prevent the doors from locking? Was he able to gain entry (perhaps on collection of the takeouts – which both couples had partaken in) and conceal himself? Or were hotel members of staff involved (though there was no evidence to suggest as such), providing copies of the key cards for the rooms? The theories were stretching the boundaries of probability. As far as Fiennes was concerned, they'd wasted far too much time on speculation – the fact was, 'Dorian' had found his way through locked doors somehow. He didn't much care how. He closed the bathroom door on his view of the mirror.

Entering the living room, he found Simone sitting at the dining table waiting for him. As soon as he saw the expression on her face, he knew that she was in one of *those* moods.

"Please, Sim, no, I can't do this tonight."

"I really do think we need to talk."

"I'm spent, I can't do this now. We've got four homicides–"

"Look, I know, but Dan said I really should speak to you tonight, and..." She trailed off at the look on Fiennes' face.

"Who the hell is Dan?!"

"That doesn't matter, it's just...look, I need to be honest with you."

"I'm all ears."

"I've slept with other men," she blurted out.

There followed silence. Seconds ticked by. They stared across the room at each other.

"What?" was all he could manage, a strangled emission.

"I've been with other men."

"Dan?"

"No, look...who they are isn't important."

"It's important to me."

"Why?"

"What the fuck do you mean, why?"

"Please don't shout."

"What is it you're expecting here, Simone? Should I invite them round here for a drink? We'll all share stories about what it was like fucking my wife."

Simone didn't respond, simply looking down at the table.

Fiennes moved quickly across the room, pulling out the chair opposite her, fighting the sudden impulse to swing it and dash it to pieces against the wall. Instead, he sank into it. He struggled to find words, looking at the same spot at the centre of the table.

At length, straining to remain calm, he said: "Who are they?"

"I don't know."

"How can you not know?"

"It's not anyone that I know. I met them on an app."

"An app?! You signed up to a dating app! That's premeditated."

"I'm not one of your homicides, Michael, for fuck's sake."

"You sure about that? 'Cos you've sure as hell made a fucking homicide of our marriage. A dating app?"

"It's not exactly a dating app. It's called *Incognito*, for anonymous sex."

Fiennes huffed an incredulous laugh.

"How many?"

"Three, or four."

"Well, which is it? Three or four?"

"Okay, four. One guy I met twice."

Fiennes' phone was vibrating in his pocket.

"I need to get back to work."

"Go on then, get back to your precious job. You're a walking cliché. So determined to be the stereotypical cop. Never at home. Marriage in pieces. Drinking too much. It's messing with your head, all the shit you see. Don't think I didn't see what you wrote on the mirror. You can't even keep it up for your wife, it's messed you up so bad."

Fiennes stared at her, at her running mascara, the loathing in her eyes.

"Well, there it is. All my fault, is it? I made you join a shagging app, I made you arrange to meet other men. I didn't understand you, was that it? I didn't give you enough attention? Didn't make you feel like a woman so you needed another man's cock inside you to do that for you? Fuck off, Simone. You call me a walking cliché."

His phone was vibrating again. He stood up.

"You know, there's a reason stereotypes exist," he said, only half talking to Simone. "They come from somewhere, you know."

Pulling out his phone, he saw a text message from Fletch: *Call me, now.* The phone vibrated again and he accepted instantly, listening.

"On my way."

He didn't look back at Simone as he left. As he ran down the stairs, he composed a text to one of the detectives he knew was in the squad room tonight.

Find out what you can about Incognito*, the dating app.*

By the time he'd reached his third hotel in as many days, Fiennes had received his response. *Incognito,* launched three years ago, had been designed around the concept of blind dates, but had gained popularity for seeking anonymous, casual sex. Its promotional material now actively encouraged this, simultaneously targeting those with hectic lives who sought uncomplicated sex, and those with unfulfilled lives who would benefit from its secrecy. Bottom line, anonymity equals no complications. Allegedly.

The victims had taken a room on the third floor. Fiennes took the elevator, meeting the forensics team in the corridor, which had been sealed off, the hotel manager allowing use of the floor above to interview the guests staying in rooms on this floor. The room itself was notable for its discrepancies: only one body, cell phones still present, no message for Fiennes scrawled on the mirror. A critical error on the killer's part that unravelled all the usual preparation, that would be crucial in apprehending him. Nevertheless, Fiennes couldn't shake the feeling he was being played.

He called through to Fletch, who was at the hospital.

"You spoken to her?"

"Only briefly. She's very confused. Heavy pain relief. She'll lose her sight in one eye. Lucky for her one of the other guests found her on the floor in the corridor when he did."

"I need to speak to her."

"I'll see if they'll let me in to her. We got the info back on Dorian. Both parents are still around, got someone tracking their address. Articles also mentioned a sister, we'll find her too."

There were some muffled conversations, hospital staff sounding unhappy, then the background noise came into focus and Fletch was speaking.

"Jenna, one of my colleagues, Detective Fiennes, would like to speak to you for a moment."

"Hello, Jenna. Don't worry, I'm not going to ask you to go over everything that happened. Detective

Fletcher has already told me. I'm interested to know how you came to be at the hotel."

Jenna replied slowly, as if carefully trying out her voice, still affected by fear and shock, stuttering with the pain and the dulling of the painkillers.

"We'd planned to meet...spend the evening together."

"Can you tell me your friend's name?"

"I'm sorry...I can't."

"Is that because you don't know it?"

Silence.

"Jenna, we're not judging your actions or your choices. We just need to understand the facts."

"No, I don't know her name. Didn't. I met her online...well...on an app."

"*Incognito*?"

"Yes."

"Can you explain how the app works?"

"You match based on specific criteria...like age, gender, sexuality...what you're into. We are all numbers. We don't exchange names or personal information. If you exchange photos, the software blurs out faces. You can arrange to meet in a neutral place...never even know each other's names."

"And you matched?"

"Yes...about five weeks ago."

"Whose suggestion was the location to meet?"

"Hers."

"And the suggestion to share a meal?"

"Hers."

"The date?"

"Hers. It was the soonest she was available."

Fiennes fell silent, thinking it through carefully. What better way to control each variable?

"She was dead…when I got out of the shower. She'd put her…in the closet. She was in the bed and I thought it was her."

"Sorry. She?"

"Yes. She might have been muscular…and was obviously wearing extra padding under the clothes to hide her breasts…but, I'm certain."

"You're talking about the person who assaulted you?"

"Yes."

"Fletch, we've been looking at this all wrong." The pieces were tumbling into place in Fiennes' mind, as he paced the hotel corridor. "All along, we've assumed we are looking for a man. But, of course, we would. The killer led us to make that assumption, killing two men as her first victims and signing off the killings as Dorian."

"So who?" Fletch had switched off the loudspeaker.

"Dorian's sister, it has to be. She's seducing them, Fletch. Casual hook-ups pose too many variables. She had to get to know them, find out what made them tick, take advantage of their loneliness. Using her anonymity to pair them off and control everything they plan to do. We'll find all six of them have been talking to the same number. People don't address each other with numbers, so there was little danger of her plan being found out when she arranged for them to meet. They were all anonymous to her too. We believed she was trying to conceal their identities, but none of them ever had identities to her in the first place. They were pawns."

"I'll get an APB out on her immediately."

"What was their surname, Fletch?"

He fell quiet as he consulted his messages. Then a longer, deeper, period of silence.

"Fletch?"

"Family name, Lawrence. Dorian Lawrence. His sister, Danielle Lawrence."

"Dan."

"It can't be," Fletch said. "Surely–"

"I need to go." Fiennes was already running down the corridor for the stairwell.

Arriving at his apartment block, Fiennes hurriedly punched in the access code at the entrance doors. The lights were out in the lobby and the stairwell beyond. It was 3:00AM; they shouldn't be out. He tried the light switches, but they didn't work.

He pulled out his Glock, aiming the sidearm ahead of him as he began to ascend the stairs, as quickly as would still allow him to assess what lay ahead, aiming upwards in front of him at every turn. Thankfully, residents would not be frequenting the communal areas at this time. Visibility was poor to non-existent.

Reaching his own apartment, he found the door ajar. He carefully pushed it open with his foot, aiming the gun ahead of him into the blackness. The lights were out here too. She must have gained access to the fuse box for the entire building.

He peered into the bathroom, catching reflection of his own movement in the mirror. He moved on, into the kitchen, finding it empty. The door to the living room was shut. He returned to the hallway to enter the living room from there. He turned the handle carefully, pushing open the door and aiming his weapon ahead of him, sweeping the room. The door to the kitchen remained shut. At the dining table, he could make out the silhouette of a person, sitting still and quiet in the dark. Beyond them was the bedroom door, standing open.

"Police! Show me your hands."

The silhouette remained impassive. Fiennes repeated the command, greeted with silence still. He began to circle the room in a wide arc, his back to the wall, moving around to line up to the side of the person sitting at the table. He could see the void of the mask covering their head.

"Give it up, Lawrence." His voice shook, loud and jarring in the early morning quiet. "The cavalry's on its way."

There was no movement from the silhouette at the table.

As Fiennes came in line with the couch between them, he could see a second person, prostrate between couch and coffee table. Their hands were bound, head also covered with a mask. Fiennes kept his gun trained on the seated figure.

"What have you done to her, Lawrence?"

Neither woman moved. Moving forward, Fiennes kept his gun pointed at the dining table, reaching down with his left hand to the woman on the ground, feeling under the mask, searching for a pulse. He found it, strong under his fingers, relief flooding through him.

His hand returned to supporting the hand holding the gun, advancing on the table.

"You could have just kept going, but you just had to show us how clever you were, didn't you? The murders were practically perfect. We were just going around in circles; you might never have been linked. But you had to talk about Dorian, had to try to tell me that you knew me."

"Haven't you worked it out yet?"

So intent was he on the person at the table, he was too late to react to the movement behind him, feeling the barrel of a gun against his neck as the woman on the floor moved quickly.

"Drop it," she hissed.

Closing his eyes in defeat, Fiennes let go of his gun, hearing it thud to the floor.

"What have you done to her?" Fiennes eyed the rigid figure on the table.

"Never mind her. She cheated on you, Mike. She was worse than all of them."

"What is it I haven't worked out, Dani? Go on, take your last opportunity to gloat."

She moved around into his field of vision, no longer wearing the mask.

"All cats look grey in the dark. You still just don't know." She kept her gun trained on him. "When Dorian died, it devastated me. Up until then, I'd thought life was all about having fun and being selfish. I learnt the hard way that we are all responsible for others. My parents never forgave me."

"Dorian killed himself."

"I was supposed to be looking after him. He'd been so upset that day, so detached in the evening. Like he'd given up. I knew he had reached rock bottom. But I wasn't going to let that affect my plans, so I went out anyway. I found him hanging from the banisters when I got home."

"So you blamed yourself?"

"Not just myself, Mike." She approached, jutting her gun into his cheek. He could see the startling glow of her eyes even in the dark. "Even now, you don't know, do you? You didn't recognise me when I joined Homicide. I realised you probably never even knew who I was back then. Anonymous, faceless, blind. But my brother died because I was losing my virginity to the school Lothario in the back of his car."

Fiennes was speechless. Him and Lawrence? It was with crushing clarity and shame that he realised he couldn't remember her because the scenario she'd just described had happened so many times.

All cats look grey in the dark.

I learnt the hard way that we are all responsible for others.

The door suddenly crashed in, a shot rang out. Seizing the opportunity, Fiennes lashed out and knocked the gun from Lawrence's hands. She jumped away from him and vaulted over the dining table. He caught a glimpse of metal in the dark as he grabbed his gun from where he'd dropped it on the floor. Taking aim, he fired two shots and she jack-knifed, followed by the shattering of glass.

Torch beams lit the room and Fiennes ran to Simone, finding she was bound to the chair, a splint running up her back to her head, secured with rope around her neck under the mask to prevent her head falling forward. She was unconscious, apparently having sustained no injury. Paramedics came in behind the flood of officers.

Fiennes retreated to the broken window, looking down to the sidewalk below. Where he expected to see Lawrence's body were only bloody flagstones.

Fiennes got home, sinking gratefully into an easy chair. They had successfully wrapped up two cases today, two men now residing in the cells awaiting prosecution. He and Simone had started divorce proceedings, their amicable separation now three months past.

The team had searched for Lawrence, convinced she couldn't have escaped a great distance, but there had been no trace of her. Eventually, they had to stop looking. There had been too much speculation, far too much time spent analysing theories as to how she could have survived two bullets and a fall from a third-storey window. Only he and Simone had had little trouble believing it to be possible. Detective Danielle Lawrence was cunning, resourceful and determined, a lethal combination in any criminal.

The only element he allowed himself to ponder over was the message in his own bathroom mirror. Confession or accusation? Perhaps both.

He knew it wasn't over. She may have disappeared, but he knew one day he would alight from the shower and see those thirteen letters again – and in them would be reflected the flash of a blade. He tried not to dwell on whether or not he would survive their final encounter. After all, he told himself, the Grim Reaper was coming for us all.

BLUEBELL

The decaying remnants of a life long ago lived stood at the peak of a gentle slope, descending to a field at the front and woodland at the rear. The church tower and lopsided walls framed the façade, while the ghost of the moon's glow filtered through the cracked stonework. Stars winked through hollow windows.

The wind strummed the weeds and grass that had grown around the gravestones that lined the inner wall of the garth like soldiers. Percussive against the weathered stone, it drummed its beat along with a whistling accompaniment through the cracks in the crumbling stone.

So it had stood and played its melodies for centuries, more shrivelled year by year, but ever present. Sometimes, it sounded as if nature's tunes were accompanied by a choir singing, the harmony not of the wind, but voices, once human but no longer. In years past, the locals steered clear of the ruins by night, still wary by day.

As the years fell away, the fear was forgotten, relegated to myth, the choir now a campfire tale. Many sought out the ruins to listen for it. Few could claim honestly to have heard it.

So it was that many a still night lit by the moon would not be greeted by music or the voices of a choir. The wind rocked against the plants, rustling tree branches, leaves floating to the ground. The moonlight shone through the broken roof and walls, lighting the windowless voids from within. In a rear window, a shadow moved, framed in the moonlight. Its shape appeared human, perhaps possessed by something that once was. But there was no one there to see it.

Golden leaves crunched underfoot and the chilly autumnal air was sharp and brisk. The leaves swirled around David as he tucked his hands into his coat pockets. Something hurled at the back of his neck and he reached into his collar to feel what it was, withdrawing a brittle leaf. He let it drift back into the wind, looking around to check no one had thrown it to get his attention. It had felt as if it was driven by more force than this evening's slothful wind. But there was no one around, the wind the only potential culprit.

He checked his watch. He was going to be early. He should not be too early, he considered, else he would look too keen, which may be discouraging. What were all these games you have to play? He felt rusty and out-of-touch, all this overthinking so alien to him even in his mid-thirties. He'd changed his shirt three times before leaving the house, regretting having not updated his wardrobe in several years.

Truth be told, he was still unsure if he was ready for this. Though it had been several years since he'd arrived home to find his wife's suitcases awaiting her departure in the hallway, the memory of that night still pained him. Sometimes he felt she was still there, looking over his shoulder. He shouldn't feel guilty for trying to move on – it was she who left him, after all – but he had never really got used to being single. Yet, here he was.

He had noticed Emily before – of course he had – always in such a rush, sweeping her shoulder-length blond hair away from her face with ringless fingers, pushing her glasses back up to the bridge of her dainty nose. She was pretty in a quiet way, the hint of freckles, a generous curve to her mouth, her green eyes her most striking feature. Watching her collect her morning coffee became as much a part of his daily routine as walking through the park or savouring the ten minutes of peace as he drank his own coffee in the corner of the coffee shop.

One morning, something unusual had occurred. Instead of rushing in and out, she had sat down at a table, eagerly opening a magazine and flicking through the pages until she came to the article she wanted to read. He realised that he was staring and quickly looked away. She was beautiful. It was something he'd not thought about a woman for a long time. Not since…

Standing at the top of the steep steps that descended into the park, he leaned on the railing and looked across the field towards the ruins of St. Monica's Priory. A magpie soared across his vision, perching atop the crumbling stone. Dusk was settling. A few children in costumes were already meandering, hoping to be amongst the first to take advantage of the dying light.

David checked his watch again and walked slowly down the steep steps into the park below. As the monastery swallowed the last morsel of daylight, he didn't notice the murder of magpies gathering on the roof and window ledges; maybe seven of them in total, if anyone could see well enough to count them, or perhaps eight or nine. By this time, there could have been any number sheltered in the recesses of the stone.

Emily checked her reflection in the hall mirror, unsure why she felt so nervous. It was just a meal. She dated infrequently, never developing more than a passing interest; she could see no reason why this occasion would be any different. Though it did feel...different, somehow. Her life was full – perhaps the work/life balance veering towards the unhealthy, but full nonetheless – it would take something, someone, very different to encourage her to change it.

She sent a text message to Chloe, saying she was leaving now and would message her later, and tucked her phone into her bag. The taxi was already parked outside. She got in and gave the name and street of the restaurant. Her choice, selected on the spur of the moment. That alone made her smile. David seemed like the perfect gentleman.

She had seen him a few times in the coffee shop, calm and placid on the corner table, gazing out of the window wistfully or people-watching within the shop. She found his stillness attractive. She wished her life allowed her moments like that. He was handsome, not in the way of a Greek demi-god of chiselled features and bulging musculature, but in a scholarly, gentle way. She realised how much she liked his face.

It had been several days since they'd spoken for the first time. There'd been an ease to their conversation, an immediate familiarity; it felt as if he had always been present. She supposed that he had – she had probably become subconsciously aware of his presence in the background of her morning routine long before she first noticed him in his corner. It was strange at times, how the brain worked. Some theories would put all of that down to chemical reactions. Was that all we were? Chemicals creating emotions, impulses creating thoughts? Or was there more to us than flesh and blood and bone?

The barista had called out her order – pumpkin spice latte to go. Both she and David had approached the counter. The barista, visibly cringing, smiled at them both awkwardly.

"Apologies, sir, this is your order. Just a few more moments, Madam."

David smiled at Emily. "Go on," he said. "You take it. I've got a few minutes to spare."

"No, I'm fine waiting, really. Thank you."

"I insist." He handed her the coffee. "I hope you have a good day, Miss?"

She couldn't help but smile. "Emily. And thank you?"

"David." He was still smiling at her. Then something seemed to occur to him. "Actually, er, Emily, I don't suppose you fancy meeting for a drink sometime? Or a meal?"

She was a little taken aback.

"Sorry, I don't make a habit of accosting women in coffee shops."

"No, it's…Yes, I'd like that."

"When are you free?"

"Thursday?" She didn't really consider that today was Monday, afterwards wondering if she looked too keen suggesting they meet in just three days.

"Thursday would be perfect. Where would you like to go?"

"How about *The Castle*?"

"I'll book a table. See you there, 7:30?"

"Perfect." She felt herself flush.

"Pumpkin spice latte to go," called the barista. David took his coffee gratefully.

"Thank you, again," Emily said, turning to leave. She realised she was still smiling halfway down the street.

David checked his watch again. It was only 7:25. It had been 7:24 when he last checked. Mist had fallen with the dusk. In the distance, the shape of the ruins was barely still visible. Headlights approached, but the car drove on. He started to feel a little foolish. Emily may be unable to come, or may have said yes only to be polite. *Polite?* How in the hell would that have been polite? He shook his head. Emily wasn't that sort of woman. It would have been sensible to swap phone numbers, but that hadn't felt right for the moment. Nor had frequenting the coffee shop in the intervening days felt the right thing to do. He'd known all along he was in danger of overthinking this, yet it seemed he had barged headlong into that trap.

He thought wistfully of a chance at a new beginning. He thought he was finally ready to love again. His heart felt alive in his chest, bursting to feel warmth and affection after so long healing inside its cold and brittle shell. He had probably pinned too much hope on Emily now, swayed by her pretty face and warm personality. Bloody fool.

Another car approached, its headlight sweeping across the field opposite as it stopped and reversed into a space. Someone was standing in the field, staring in the direction of the restaurant, at him waiting outside. He shifted his feet, feeling self-conscious. The scrutiny felt invasive.

Headlights filled the road again and a taxi stopped in front of the restaurant. He smiled warmly as Emily got out from the back seat.

"You look amazing."

"Thank you." She blushed.

He held out his arm to motion her to enter the restaurant ahead of him. As they walked through the doorway, he glanced back to the opposite side of the road. Someone stood on the pavement, a wraith-like figure with long, dark hair covering their face, dressed in ragged clothing. Slowly, an arm raised, a finger pointed at him.

They were greeted at the door by the restaurant manager. Disconcerted, David explained they had a booking for a table for two. He glanced back out through the glass door. The wraith-like figure had gone.

A young, curly-haired waitress led them to their table. David pulled out a chair for Emily and then sat opposite, each taking the menus proffered by the waitress. David gasped sharply.

"What's wrong, David?"

"It's nothing, really." But he was flustered, seemingly preoccupied with the table's centrepiece – a vase of artificial bluebells, in full bloom as fake flowers often are.

They discussed the restaurant. David hadn't been here before, Emily only once. Perusing the menu, they weighed up choices, remarking how delicious some of the dishes sounded. An ease developed in their conversation. Emily was relieved that David had relaxed following his tension when they first came in.

They selected a bottle of red wine, which the waitress promptly brought to their table and poured. Ordering their starters and main courses, they sipped from their glasses and settled into conversation, which began at the coffee shop.

David realised how difficult it was to avoid the subjects he imagined could be potential mood-killers or sensitive areas – work and family, or, the death toll of a first date, past relationships – while talking about their lives and where they lived. He doubted they could be avoided; he certainly wasn't sure how it would be possible. He alluded to his ex-wife when talking about their house, then moved on, hoping he'd not said the wrong thing.

They were discussing films when their starters arrived – Emily had goat's cheese marinated in beetroot, with a side salad; David had duck liver pate and toasted brioche. The food was delicious; both were satisfied with their choices.

"So, what do you do?" Emily asked, turning the conversation to work.

"I'm an architect. I work for a local company, Sullivan's. How about you?"

"I work at the local paper. I'm a journalist – in fact, I want to branch into investigative journalism, that's what I'm working towards." She finished her glass of wine. "Please excuse me for a minute."

David relaxed a little as she left the table. He was preoccupied, staring at the bluebells. Every year, on the anniversary of the day his wife left him, he received a single bluebell, left on the step in a deliberate attempt to remind him, to prevent him moving on. Finally he'd met someone and wanted to give moving on a chance, and here were a whole bunch of them.

He looked beyond the bluebells, to Emily's vacated seat. For a fleeting moment, he wondered if she would not return, as this evening was already descending rapidly to disastrous. Something moved beyond his vision, a blur of rags. He raised his head.

The wraith leered at him from the darkened street, fingers tapering against the glass as its hand reached out to him. The flesh of its face was cracked, falling away from the bone in strips, as ragged as its clothes. Long, bedraggled hair framed its face, falling to merge with the tatters that cloaked its shoulders. There was a plea in its eyes, something calling out to him, a scream from beyond the veil...

Emily sat down. David visibly flinched. Concern flashed across her face before she recovered her smile.

"You look like you've seen a ghost."

With effort, David laughed. Emily tried not to allow it to make her feel awkward. She was surprised at how much she was enjoying the evening so far. She liked David; they clicked on a level she found rare on first dates. Yet there was something haunted about him, an underlying pre-occupation that she thought likely was connected to his ex-wife. Paradoxically, that made her more interested. She felt sympathy for him. Her attraction to damaged souls was inescapable.

David finished his glass of wine, struggling to ignore the aura of terror that had embraced him, like Death itself was reaching up from the base of his spine to drag him into the depths. He smiled at Emily, her delicate features, her intelligent, green eyes, sparkling with life.

"Back to what we were talking about – do you have a passion project?" David asked. "Something for your first investigation?" He reached for the bottle of wine.

"Well, actually yes, I do have a dream project." Emily sipped from her replenished glass. "A series of articles. I've called it *Hauntings and Histories*, a series of investigations into allegedly haunted locations in the context of their history, but with the perspective that our modern culture and recent history may throw upon it. Maybe it's a bit of a pipe dream, but I'm already working on the first article."

"That sounds really interesting." David was genuinely enthusiastic, glad they had found something they could discuss in detail that would prove a distraction from his troubled thoughts. "What's the first article about?"

"St. Monica's Priory."

Their main courses were served with a flourish. Emily had ordered pumpkin ravioli with sage-browned butter sauce; David a ribeye steak with peppercorn sauce. Again, they remarked positively on the food, before Emily resumed the topic of the article she was writing.

"The monastery seemed to dominate my life when I was a little girl. I studied it in history lessons,

136

in religion, in art. I visited it on school trips, and remember drawing the stained-glass windows in my sketchbook. We used to put pieces of paper against stone plaques and gravestones, shading over it so we could try to decipher what the inscriptions said. I played there with my friends, though our parents tried to stop us going there when they found out. As a teenager, I even had my first kiss there, while walking hand in hand with my crush amongst the ruins. It's probably fair to say it's become almost an obsession.

"It was built in the 13th century, estimated between 1237 and 1241. According to records, between thirty and fifty Benedictine monks lived there at any one time. Education and recruitment to the Church were very important at the Priory, so they also housed novices, who were fifteen plus, and children, who were called oblates. Many of the Priory's novices would move on to the nearby abbeys. I haven't been able to find any record of the number who may have stayed with the Priory. One who did was Brother Lucas. The third son of a local landowner, he joined the Priory as a novice, and stayed for many years, ultimately becoming its youngest Prior, a position he held until its dissolution."

David listened attentively while he ate his meal. Emily told her story slowly, between mouthfuls of food, after he had to remind her to keep eating, her passion for her subject evident.

"To all intents and purposes, St. Monica's was dedicated to worship and learning, a closed-off community that nevertheless supported the wider locale through spiritual endeavours and employment opportunities. But..." Emily took another mouthful and chewed her food politely. "I think there was something darker hidden beneath the surface." She smiled at the waitress as she approached, asking if everything was okay with their meals. They were both complimentary and David ordered a second bottle of wine. They resumed eating, the waitress soon back at the table and refilling their glasses.

"You were saying, about the dark secret?" David prompted.

"I'll come to explain how I came to that conclusion. It actually has its origin in my own childhood. But it makes sense to keep running through its history first."

David nodded.

"Brother Lucas was the Priory's final prior. Henry VIII's desire to divorce and remarry led to the Act of Supremacy and the break from the Roman Catholic Church, and the creation of the Anglican Church, in 1534. I always found it ironic that the country's dominant faith, even to this day, was built on the bedrock of sin." She was smiling, a twinkle in her eye. "Christianity still outranks atheism by more than double its number of believers; Anglicanism the dominant denomination. Henry VIII declared himself the supreme head of the Church of England, a tradition that continues to this day under Elizabeth II.

"Of course, it wasn't plain sailing for this new Church. Politics and religion have always made uneasy bedfellows. Under the short reign of Edward VI, there were many Protestant reforms, moving the new Church away from Catholic doctrine, while Mary I attempted to reverse all those reforms and return to the Catholic faith. Only under Elizabeth I, with a new Act of Supremacy, was the independence re-established, though, naturally, dispute and turmoil continued. Protestantism versus Catholicism is as constant a war as the battle over the country of Israel, from the English Civil Wars to 20th century Ireland. Islam has been demonised in the 21st century due to fundamentalism and terrorism, yet it appears to be a malignancy common to all Abrahamic faiths. Though it's worth noting, religion alone is rarely the trigger for war.

"But, back to history. Following Elizabeth, James I ascended to the English thrown. The time under his rule was also incredibly significant for religion. The Authorised King James translation of the Bible is still in use to this day. And how can the significance of the Gunpowder Plot be ignored, an assassination attempt on the King by a Catholic group. But it wasn't only Catholics who became persecuted at this time. James believed he was being plotted against by witches, leading to numerous witch trials, amongst the most famous being in Lancashire in 1612. Of course…"

She laughed, taking a long sip from her wine glass. Their plates were set aside.

"I'm sorry, I'm completely digressing from the point." The wine had gone to her head by now, she realised.

"No, it's very interesting." David laughed with her.

"Nevertheless, I'm supposed to be telling you about Brother Lucas. The witch trials are stories for another day. St. Monica's was in ruins by then. Though we can well imagine the legends that may

139

have arisen about it from such a paranoid time in history."

"I look forward to those future stories."

She smiled, resisting the sudden urge to lace her fingers through his, their hands close on the tablecloth.

"Anyhow, the Suppression Acts followed, and the monasteries began to be closed. They had amassed so much wealth and power over the centuries and Henry couldn't allow the Catholic dominance to continue. St. Monica's could not escape it, but Brother Lucas was not willing to give up without a fight. Their resistance was futile. The monastery was attacked and vandalised in 1538. Brother Lucas was hanged, drawn and quartered inside the monastery walls, his body set on fire along with the building itself. His remains were purported to have been buried somewhere on the grounds."

"That's brutal."

"Yes. Human history is bloody." She smiled as David poured them each a final glass of wine. The waitress approached, clearing away their plates and asking if they wished for desserts. They both ordered.

"Ever since then, St. Monica's has stood empty, while tales of supernatural phenomena have persisted as much as its structure. I experienced some of it myself. As a small child, I saw the flames. My mother told me it was an illusion created by the red sky of the morning. I was never so sure."

Their desserts arrived – both had ordered a caramel and white chocolate cheesecake. They both finished their glasses of wine.

"I heard the woman crying when I was a child too. My most chilling memory. Many have reported hearing her cry. It's been suggested they are the echo of the night the monastery was raided. I remember the crying of one woman. She would prove to be the cornerstone of my work. It's what started the idea in my head and why I believe St. Monica's and Brother Lucas to hide a dark secret."

David waited.

"A woman crying. It was a monastery. For men. Why was a woman there?"

"I see what you're saying."

"I've spent years researching local history, visiting museums and scouring their archives of medieval manuscripts and volumes. With a bit of conjecture and study of local legend, I was able to put together a hypothesis – several women apparently disappeared in this area over a period of several years in the early 16th century. However vague these records are, they did not continue after 1538."

David was amazed.

"You think you've solved an historical serial murder case?"

"I'm nowhere near being able to support that. But I believe Brother Lucas was responsible for those women's disappearances. It's not just religious turmoil that has persisted throughout history. Powerful, corrupt organisations, protecting powerful men who abuse and harm women and children. We know the Church has form for it, and nothing has illustrated the continued abuse of women by powerful men in recent times than the revelations of the #MeToo movement. Truth will out! Even royalty and politicians aren't immune. But what I want to be able to do with my articles is to use a combination of historical, paranormal and forensic investigation to get as close to the truth as possible."

"You tell a remarkable story," David said.

"I'm sorry, I got so carried away," Emily laughed sheepishly.

"No, don't apologise, I've really enjoyed tonight."

"Perhaps next time you can have the floor, tell me more about you."

"I'd like that. Next time, that is, rather than having the floor. You'll find me not nearly as interesting as you are."

"Now, I don't think that's true. Though, I must admit, I do like a man of mystery."

"Something else to solve?"

"Something like that."

They ordered coffees, the restaurant around them getting steadily quieter.

"Tell me something," David said after a little time. "Do you believe in the paranormal phenomena you investigate? Ghosts?"

She was thoughtful for a moment.

"I certainly want to. And I don't discount any of the experiences that people have reported. But are we, on some level, interpreting these things how we want to interpret them rather than as they actually are? As much as we may fear it, do we not, deep down in our DNA, want it to be true? For all our progress, there's one thing we cannot conquer. Really, don't we want to know that our loved ones and, ultimately, ourselves will continue to exist beyond our deaths, to live forever? Truthfully, I don't know what to think." She sipped her coffee, still hot. "What do you think?"

Rising unbidden, the wraith reached for him from memory.

"I've always been sceptical," was his reply. "To the point that I don't believe the half of what I hear. In general, it feels as if we can't trust anything we hear or read or even see anymore. Which seems crazy in an age when anyone can have a voice."

"I know what you mean. One thing can so easily turn into another and these things escalate so quickly, no one really knows what the original point was. It makes it easier to claim something is fake news amongst so much hyperbole, reactive emotion and fear-mongering. So many people are keyboard terrorists. I've seen colleagues take advantage of it time and time again, selecting what they want to publish to convey a certain impression from a wealth of quotes available without having to go to the effort of interviewing anyone."

"It strikes me as pretty lazy journalism to simply copy negative comments from social media to string an article together."

"Welcome to the modern tabloid."

They laughed.

"Every so often," David continued. "Someone or something a little more trustworthy may come along, which makes me question what may or may not be out there. Your story of seeing the monastery on fire, all these centuries later, seems all too credible." He finished his coffee. "Who knows, maybe it's just tonight, seeing all the costumes earlier this evening."

"There could be something in that," Emily agreed. "On this night, when the veil between the living and the dead is at its thinnest. There is something spiritually potent about the eve of a holy day, a new beginning, or a change in season. All Hallows' Eve, Christmas Eve, even the eve of a new year. Keep going back through history and you will keep finding different versions of these traditions, the timing almost exact. Samhain. Yule. Of course, there's an element of traditions being adopted and names changed to manipulate people into observing them. But I like to think there's also something organic about it. So much energy, the pain of death and the agony of rebirth."

David held her gaze for a long time. His brown eyes were gentle in his strong, clean-shaven face. She felt as if she wanted to say something, but couldn't find the words. She looked down into the dregs of her coffee.

"Perhaps ghosts are just a snapshot of old memories, old emotions, like a crackly phonograph, a crumpled photograph, a grainy video film. Sometimes events and influences are so visceral that they leave a mark on the world, like a scar that doesn't fully heal. Scars that may ache or burn or still suffer pain, long after the cause of the damage has passed and the wound has apparently healed.

"I think some of us are more susceptible to feeling those scars than others, becoming aware of them while others feel nothing. And I think there are other factors too – time – days, seasons. For instance, Wiccans believe this veil between life and death isn't solid, but porous, at its thinnest between the hours of midnight and three o'clock, thinner still at certain times, like Samhain. Tonight. There's something about the cold dead of night in the middle of winter when the veil feels thinner, when the scars worry more."

David's eyes continued to watch her as she talked. He said nothing, waiting for her to continue.

"Some people are oblivious to the scars. Others are ultra-sensitive. Maybe most people can only feel the influence of these spiritual scars when it's close to them – family, their homes, something in their own past. Though sometimes the scar is so huge that it's inescapable, however anyone may interpret it, damage on such a scale that the entire world can feel it. How could anyone bear witness to the silence of Auschwitz and deny that?"

She finished the last of her coffee, now cold. It tasted bitter, not like the pumpkin spice latte she and David had met over.

"So I suppose, yes, I do believe in ghosts. I don't know if we're just sensing history, witnessing long-lost memories, or at what level we could actually interact with or influence what we witness. Are we interacting with a past memory or a present, existing consciousness that has survived that memory? Even if that is the case, is that the same as a person's soul? It may be a surviving fragment, or else a conscious entity that bears little or no relation to the living person that once was."

She realised she was still holding David's gaze.

"Something I am sure of. Those who are remembered, can never die."

David felt that he could listen to Emily talk for hours. He wanted to, amongst other things.

"This got deep for a first date." Emily smiled, feeling tired.

"I've had a very nice evening," David said.

"Me too."

"Let me give you my number. Maybe we can do this again." He retrieved his phone from his pocket, brought up his own number and placed the phone on the table in front of Emily. He asked for the bill as she typed his number into her own phone. He heard the buzz as she dialled him and hung up.

"Shall we split it down the middle?"

He refused. "I'll get this."

"My treat next time then."

Their waitress brought over the card machine and they thanked her. The bill paid, including a tip for the waitress, they stood to leave, David helping Emily into her coat. He rested his hands on her shoulders momentarily. They walked outside.

The air was bitter, their skin immediately flushed. The mist had grown thick, the streetlights glowing like orbs. The moon was full, piercing the mist. David opened the rear door of a nearby taxi for Emily.

"I hope to see you again," he said, unsure how they should say goodbye.

They held each other's eyes for a few moments, moving to kiss the other's cheek. Their lips met instead, a tender, exploratory kiss. They broke away, eyes locked again.

"Thank you for a lovely evening," Emily told him, getting into the taxi. He closed the door, standing back as it pulled away from the curb.

He considered walking home, but instead got himself a taxi. His phone vibrated in his pocket.

Looking forward to next time already x

Glancing up, he saw a dark shape on the pavement as the taxi rushed past it. He looked back.

The wraith was pointing at him, rags dragging in the road, before it was swallowed up by the mist.

Emily pondered as the taxi headed for her home. Something had clicked with David, but she wasn't going to pretend she knew precisely what. She felt foolish sending the message so soon, even more foolish when she found herself checking if he had replied yet.

Changing her mind, she asked the driver to stop where they were, paid for her journey so far, and got out on to the pavement, bracing herself against the cold. She'd drunk too much; she was feeling romantic and sentimental about an evening spent in the company of a stranger. But it didn't feel that way and she didn't want him to remain one.

She ought to focus her mind. She'd gone down this path before with damaged men; it always ended with her tears. Work would be her salvation, not sentiment and daydreams. Huddled into her coat, regretting already not having continued on her journey home in the warm taxi, she looked across the park to the hulking grey mass of St. Monica's Priory. It called to her across the centuries.

A lone car drove slowly down the street, the driver inquisitive about the woman standing alone on the pavement. She ignored his gaze and turned to enter the park via the gate, crunching through leaves already thick with frost. She had almost shared with David her idea to continue her investigation tonight. But this was something she needed to do alone. Her article was almost finished. But there was something lacking. That final experience, something to further illustrate her suspicions. She hoped a visit on Hallowe'en night would complete it.

The wind ruffled around her, jostling leaves against her legs as she walked across the grass. The clouds moved high overhead, allowing only brief glimpses of the moon. She glanced back at the well-lit street behind her, framed by the black-iron fencing, now no more than a haze in the mist. Adversely, the light and the people did not always seem the safer place to be.

The spectre of St. Monica's was unflinching up ahead. In darkness, it appeared to grow in stature, to loom into the night sky with a malevolence that crumbling stone and cracked glass could not muster by daylight. A whoop of laughter made her jump. She heard distant running. Probably teenagers, she thought. But, still, she considered turning away, craving the warmth of home, where she could watch a late-night film on TV and enjoy some chocolate.

She neared the outer wall, tendrils of mist appearing to cling to the top of it. The light was far away now. The wind wrapped the cold around her. The stone archway towered over her head and she paused beneath it, where huge doors had once stood to bar access to the outside world. Now the monastery's secrets were for all to find, if they could decipher the clues left under the weight of years gone by.

She checked her phone, seeing she no longer had any signal. The time blinked at her. 23:57. She pushed the phone deep into her coat pocket.

The hush felt heavier beyond the archway, within the monastery grounds. The church building towered above her; the top of the bell tower no longer visible. The church survived to a greater extent than the rest of the monastery. Catholicism had still held tight in the beliefs and practices of the dislocated Church. Those attacking the monastery could still not bring themselves to destroy its spiritual heart.

The doorway lay open, its door long crumbled to dust. She looked into the nave beyond. Plant life had invaded, claiming back the earth. Their shapes were just distinguishable. Emily wondered if she was witnessing the future as well as the past. One day, when humanity has become dust, nature will reclaim the planet, and humanity's destructiveness will have claimed only one casualty – itself.

Emily stared upwards, at the cross atop the tower, a symbol of resurrection and hope. She had once come here, an evening when she was far more drunk than she was now, fearing the loss of the first man she had loved. She had begged for a sign, screaming to the heavens to prove there was indeed hope, praying through tears to God to not abandon her here. The night had remained still; cold and lonely. She had not been able to tell David the truth tonight, not fully. As an adult, St. Monica's had been an empty void. She could no longer feel its scars.

She rounded the church, slipping through a crevice in the stone wall, into the cloister. All that remained were the stone pillars framing the central grassed area – the garth, once the monastery garden and graveyard, only the relics of ancient headstones remaining. She'd knelt before them on so many occasions, the hands of a child tracing the weathered lettering, names lost to time, never to be known again.

At the far end of the graveyard, walls crumbled almost to the ground, where the refectory and communal rooms had once stood. Only brittle shadows remained of this section of the monastery. Between the church and refectory had been the east and west ranges – the east behind the garth; the west before it, scarcely anything left other than the wall through which she'd gained access to the cloister. Henry's rebels had battered their way through the west range entrance to gain entry to the monastery's inner sanctum.

Emily rounded the cloister, stopping where the chapter house had once been, flanked by the library and scriptorium. How much knowledge had burned that night when faith was challenged? When they brought down the west range, where the sick and the dying would have lain in the infirmary, where guests would have slept in their beds, the monks would have known what fate awaited them. Did they remain in their beds, or rise to meet the fight head on, or did they congregate in the church to ask for God's mercy? Why did He not reach out to save them?

Emily closed her eyes, the mist and darkness tightening around her. She sighed. This was no investigation. She was fooling herself. It was time to go home. Waiting here in the darkest hours of All Saints' Day in the shadow of millennia, hoping for a sign from the universe to show her that existence had a higher purpose, that all that was lost was never truly gone. This had as much to do with her dating again as it did her work. Couldn't she just be normal? She needed a sign to let her put her faith in a man.

She turned around to leave the way she had come, glimpsing movement in the doorway to the sacristy, now only a shell of stone and weeds. She squinted. A human shape hovered in the archway; torn rags blown by the wind. Movement again, as if an arm was reaching up.

A light caught her eye, floating beyond a stained-glass window of the church. She looked back to the sacristy archway. No human shape, only the barely discernible trees that had conquered the shell. But the light still hovered in the church, steady, like the glow of a lantern moving between the pews, casting light up to the window, the choir of monks having been awakened to gather to sing Nocturns; Brother Lucas moving between them to check all were present. A trick of the light, the moon through the mist and coloured by a stained-glass window.

The wind whipped up around her again, howling through crevices. It carried with it the sound of voices, a low chorus, a haunting melody from centuries gone by.

David had attempted to sleep and failed. He'd contemplated how to reply to Emily's message, but he couldn't bring himself to do it. He could not shake free of that night, when suitcases had been packed and she had left him.

Every time he closed his eyes, the wraith drifted across his vision, reaching for him with hands of decaying flesh, flaying in strips from the bone. A maggot rolled out of its eye.

He got out of bed, boiled the kettle and then changed his mind, poured a glass of brandy instead. Finally, he got dressed and left the house.

The voices echoed around the interior of the church. Acapella, a chorus of the lost and lonely, distant, audible down the centuries. Emily closed her eyes and absorbed it, almost feeling the words in the mist around her. Nocturns may have been the only time the monks used their voices in company, many obeying a vow of silence in the lit hours. Here, under cover of darkness, they rejoiced in the glory of God.

She walked around to the church entrance, the voices shrinking, as if getting further away. Standing in the archway, she looked into the abandoned nave; its empty, broken pews; the plant life that rose through the cracked stone floor. The moonlight shone through one of the stained-glass windows, lighting up St. Monica herself, reaching out a hand to lead the faithless and those led astray to salvation.

Emily's shoes scuffed on the stone floor as she entered. Abandoned, the church felt cold and unloved, the filtered moonlight resting on cracked stone and rotten wood. She felt the centuries of this once holy place weighing down upon her. She walked deeper into the nave. She should have brought her camera. She pulled her phone out of her pocket instead.

The hush was pierced by soft crying. She turned her head sharply to listen, memories flooding back. The same whimpering she had heard as a child. She moved to her right, stepping past cracked pews. Through a doorway were stone steps, which led up to the cells on the first floor of the east range. Stopping at the bottom of the stairs, she listened. The crying came from above.

Flicking on the flashlight app on her phone, she shone it upwards. The steps were steep. She steadied herself with her hands on the rough stone walls, unable to see where she was treading while she kept the light trained upwards. She carefully felt each step with her foot, testing with pressure before placing her entire weight on it. She was grateful when she reached the top, still shining the light ahead of her. She cursed as it blinked out, checking her phone screen. The red failing battery symbol blinked at her before the screen went black.

The moonlight was again breaking through the gaps in the walls and roof, casting deeper shadows throughout the length of the corridor. There were a dozen cells on each side of the corridor, where the monks had slept and spent time in study and reflection. A further floor of cells had once stood above this one, but was no more. She had explored each of the small rooms many times before, nothing left now of the sparse furnishings they would have featured. She continued to steady herself against the wall as she moved down the corridor, fearful that part of the floor may give way at any moment.

She stopped beside one of the doorways. The mournful crying came from within. She squinted into the dark. A shape crouched in the far corner, just visible beneath the window.

"Hello?" Emily's voice shook. "Do you need help?"

The shape moved and rose, now in view in front of the window, wearing a monk's hooded cowl.

Emily was rooted to the spot. The monk was motionless, appearing not to react to her, as if she was not there. There was something not quite solid about the monk, as if it was as one with the mist, only half visible, bathed in a silver aura in the moonlight. The hood lowered, revealing a shaved head, facing away from her, towards the window. The monk removed the robe and cowl, placing them on the bed. The monk sat beside them, back to the door, beginning to unwrap linen from around their torso.

Something moved past Emily, another shape materialising from the mist in the room. She gasped as the monk on the bed turned to look at the newcomer, their silhouette framed in the moonlight – the feminine features of their face, the curve of breasts previously hidden under the padding of linen.

"My child." A voice from the corner of the room. Male. Paternal. "You must flee."

"Has he found me, Brother?" A gentle, female voice.

"Your husband is no longer the only thing to fear. The King's men have arrived. If they find a woman in our midst, I cannot fathom what horrors they may inflict upon her. You must flee. Immediately."

"You have been so good to me, Brother Lucas. How can I ever repay your kindness?"

"Only by living your life in happiness and by the grace of our Lord, Jesus Christ."

"Will you come with me?"

"My brothers and I shall pray and await what fate has in store for us. There is nothing to fear in the arms of the Lord."

"Thank you, Brother. For everything."

"Bless you, my child."

Emily could hear the song of the choir once more, rising in defiance from below, even as distant shouts could be heard from across the park. She turned behind her, hearing the shouts growing louder, the splintering of wood, explosions, screams of terror. She turned back, the room empty, the woman departed into the mist. Had she been able to escape? A question she may never know the answer to.

A light hovered at the end of the corridor at the top of the steps, blocking her exit. The shouts and screams were louder; the ground shook beneath her feet. The crying resumed. She realised it was her own. The light moved closer, a lantern, held by a hand, emerging from a robe and cowl, a hood covering the face.

"Who are you?" the voice that had belonged to Brother Lucas asked of her.

Emily could not speak, paralysed.

"Do not be afraid. You are safe here. God will protect you."

"You were protecting them," she blurted. "They hid in plain sight, pretended to be men. No one knew the truth. Only you."

She shivered violently.

"In honour of our namesake."

Emily closed her eyes.

St. Monica. The patron of wives and victims of abuse. Leading people to the faith.

She had been blind, all too ready to see Brother Lucas as a monster. Those women were not trapped. They had found salvation.

Running footsteps sounded below, more shouting.

"You should go now," Brother Lucas told her, his light moving away. "Do not fear the path we tread. Christ will protect us." The lantern was thrown from his grasp, shattering at Emily's feet, fire flaring. Brother Lucas was pulled into the blackness. She could still hear his voice in her head.

"Those who are loved, will live forever."

The fire was taking hold, ripping through the beams of wood that had once supported the ceiling. Emily ran, tripping into the stairwell, only just managing to support herself against the wall and stop herself plummeting down the steps. She could feel the growing heat of the flames, alarm turning to panic as she tumbled into the church below and on to her knees.

Picking herself up, she ran into the aisle and towards the doorway. She stopped, skidding on the dusty stone. Someone stood in her path. They took a step towards her, lifting a hand, pointed in her direction. Still she could hear the screams and the shouting, the walls being torn down, the roar of the flames. But this figure appeared unaffected.

As the flames lit the altar behind Emily, the dark figure was illuminated, hair and rags half-decayed, tatters around the husk of a corpse. She approached Emily. Flames began to lick her rags, but still she appeared not to notice. The skin on her face was torn, her neck bruised, swollen and purple, the skin on her hands flaking.

156

With a roar, she lunged at Emily. They fell backwards, collapsing on to stone, the wraith pinning Emily down. Screams filled her head with a cacophony of torment.

"Keep away! Keep away!" Over and over again, filling her mind until she thought her eardrums would burst.

The wraith became consumed by the flames. Emily could feel the immense heat, but her skin did not burn. She fought the wraith away, the woman appearing to almost crumble off her, and dragged herself up the aisle on her knees. She turned to see the burning wraith bowed where the altar would have once stood. St. Monica reached down to the screaming soul from the stained-glass window.

Emily ran from the church and from the monastery grounds. She stumbled in the grass and fell, sobbing into the earth. She raised her head and looked back. St. Monica's was engulfed in flames, reaching high to the moonlit sky. The mist had dispersed. The stars looked on, unaffected. The heavens were untroubled by the strife of the earth.

She watched for a while, this scene she had seen before as a child. The monastery smouldered, its dying embers subsiding into time.

A woman passed her shortly, walking in the direction of the old building. Emily turned her head to look at her.

"Are you searching for something?" she asked, from where she sat on the grass. The woman jumped, as if she hadn't seen her sitting there.

"I was told I could find help here," the woman said, after a pause. She was really no more than a girl. Emily thought of Brother Lucas, of the violent end he met.

"It's gone now," she replied. "You won't find salvation here anymore."

Emily let the front door close behind her. She leaned back against it, emotionally exhausted. She should sleep, but she knew that, as soon as her head hit the pillow, she would not be able to. She caught sight of her reflection in the hall mirror. Her hair was a mess, her makeup smeared, her clothes covered in dust and mud.

She ran herself a bath. Gratefully sinking into the hot water, she closed her eyes. She would re-write her article. There was no medieval serial killer, only the sad reality that women were abused by the men they loved. Even when they managed to escape, they lived in fear of being pursued. Brother Lucas had offered them sanctuary, until he was torn down and punished for standing up for what he believed in.

When she was able to feel the tension slipping out of her limbs, she got out of the bath, drying herself and wrapping a thick dressing gown around her. Her shoulders felt sore, stinging at the touch. In front of the bedroom mirror, she studied the deep purple bruising developing. So powerful was the wraith-like woman's emotion, it had broken through the veil to leave a physical trace.

She opened her laptop and began to write. She didn't know if she would share it, but she recounted her experience and the revelation of the women's disappearances – they had shed their identities, willingly participating in monastery life, safe from the outside world and the men who sought to do them harm.

Unease still rumbled in her belly, even as she typed the final word. The wraith-like spirit kept looming out of the night, her words repeating inside Emily's head.

She checked her phone, now charging. She had received three messages – all from Chloe.

How was it? X

You dirty bitch! I'm never letting you live this down. On the FIRST date! Xx

Right, now I'm worried. Just let me know you're not dead in a ditch please xx

Emily replied: *Date was good. No, I didn't sleep with him. I'm not dead x*

Her phone rang instantly.

"Where have you been?" Chloe asked. "I've been worried."

Emily recounted the story, first of her date with David, how she'd confided in him about her project and then visited St. Monica's; how she'd witnessed ghosts from centuries past and may even have interacted with Brother Lucas, and finally her encounter with the wraith-like spectre who had managed to physically bruise her.

"All I could hear, in my head, over and over again, was 'Keep away'. It wasn't a threat; it was a warning. It felt as if she wasn't just talking about the monastery, maybe not at all about it." Something occurred to her. She opened the internet search engine on the laptop. "I don't know, just with it happening tonight of all nights..." She typed and pressed enter.

"Maybe you should take it as a sign." Chloe was never one to take anything as a sign.

Emily was silent as the search engine loaded. She selected the first result, an article from a national newspaper. The photograph loaded at the top of the page.

"I think you're right. I'm just sending you something."

She heard the ping of the email arriving on the other end of the line.

"Whoa! That's her, this wraith?"

"Yes. Minus the marks around her neck."

"You should write this. What's that quote? Men are afraid that women will laugh at them, women are afraid that men will kill them? Maybe that's what you should call the article."

"Margaret Atwood. I've got no evidence. I'll lose my credibility before I start. I'm a journalist, not a novelist. I don't write fiction; I need evidence to back up my claims."

"What's the difference? Both just make stuff up, fiction, non-fiction."

Emily said nothing, barely raising a smile at the oft-repeated joke. Tonight, she didn't have a smart comment with which to retaliate. "I need to sleep. I'll speak to you tomorrow, later today, whichever is right." She felt drained. They said goodbye and she ended the call, switching off her laptop.

After some time, she typed out a text message and pressed send before she could overthink it. She crawled under the covers, still wearing her dressing gown, and switched out the light. Finally, she felt she could succumb to sleep.

*

The sun rose behind the ruins of St. Monica's Priory, evicting the moon from its throne in the heavens. The clouds were bathed in a red hue, spreading across the skyline and framing the ancient remains, the stained-glass reflecting a crimson haze while the light dazzled through the gaps and battered stone. David could understand why a young child may look upon such a sight and imagine it ablaze.

He circled the outer wall of the ruins; just one of the early morning walkers. No one would have guessed this to be the fourth time he had taken this route while he waited for the dawn. Soon, he entered the woodland, veering away from the wall to walk between the trees. He stopped beside one, looked around him, then turned to look back at the monastery, the sun behind him now, not yet high enough to betray his position in the shadow of the trees. He was momentarily blinded by the light reflected off a rear stained-glass window of the church.

His phone vibrated and he withdrew it from his pocket. There was poor reception here; he'd had none for several hours. He read Emily's message and pocketed his phone again without composing a response. He gazed up at the monastery walls, then turned and rounded the trees, walking deeper, until he came to a fallen tree trunk. He sat on it, thoughtful.

Perhaps Emily was no great loss. She may have turned out to be like all the others. He remembered that night when he had almost tripped over the suitcases in the hallway.

"I'm leaving you," she had told him, this time determined. The tears had already been streaming down her face, leaking from her bruised eyes.

"No. You're not." He locked the front door.

"Please, David. Let me go."

"You belong with me."

"I love you, David. But we're toxic. You must see that."

He winced as he recalled the slap he'd given her. She had always pushed him, made him do terrible things.

"Who is he?"

"There's nobody else. I've told you."

He grabbed her by the shoulders.

"Stop lying, you fucking whore. Who is he?"

She cried and begged and tried to shake him loose. Struggling, they tripped over the cases she had left in the hallway. That was when he became overcome with rage.

"You're not leaving me. I can't live without you."

She would not stop crying. It really irritated him when she moaned like that. He grabbed her throat and squeezed, screaming at her to shut up.

She had got her way after all, as was always the way. She left him. He gave the contents of the cases to charity. Why should he hold on to them for her? He'd reported her missing after several weeks. But the police couldn't find a trace of her.

He sighed. Maybe next time he found someone, they'd be able to help him move on.

The sunlight filtered through the trees. He studied the ground. It remained undisturbed. He shuddered as he thought of the wraith. Is that how she looked now? He didn't like to think about it. But after such an anxious night, he realised there was nothing to fear.

A single bluebell remained, at the foot of a tree trunk. Its petals were browned and brittle, as delicate as a moth's wings. The sunshine filtered through it, a lonely elder abandoned by its long dead companions, braving the cold world in solitude. A gust of wind jostled with it. In spring, this area would be a sea of blue, hiding what lay beneath.

Mind at ease, David stood and walked away. His footsteps through the leaves and twigs faded away. Another, stronger, gust of wind blew amongst the trees. The single bluebell finally gave up the ghost, uprooted, dry petals fluttering in the air, lost to time and to memory.

'TWAS THE NIGHT BEFORE CHRISTMAS

She would always remember the first night he visited, on a cold and treacherous Christmas Eve so many years before. Not unlike this one, with the wind howling down the chimney and a young child awaiting the arrival of St. Nicholas. Through the thin glass, she watched the cobbled street, awaiting the purr of the engine and crunch of tyres, fearful of a faraway tread of hooves and wheels bouncing from the cracks.

Her fingertips touched the cold pane, as the first snowfall of winter began; flakes gently floating against the glass, vanishing as if at the touch of her fingers. That day had seen the first snowfall of winter too, while she had been walking the fields with her younger brother, her father having gone down into the village to stock up on provisions. She had raised her arms to the sky, thanking the Lord that it was to be a white Christmas.

Laughing, she and her brother had run back to the house, where they found their mother assisting Mrs Gibbon, the cook and housekeeper, with the preparations for this evening's dinner and tomorrow's celebratory luncheon. It was a tradition for their mother to help in the kitchen each Christmas; so as never to forget her roots, she said.

"Would you like any help, Mother?"

"No, thank you, Ellie. You just keep your brother occupied until your father gets home and we can prepare for this evening."

Which she dutifully did. Holidays, Christmas in particular, while they were children had been filled with games and laughter, the sheer joy that only children can feel. Reminiscing, then, had always overflowed with a warm glow, not tinged with the cold edge of sadness and the bitterness of regret. Childhood should be as sweet as candy cane and she was glad of it, but only wished she could see it otherwise than as through the glass of a snow globe.

She remembered the many Christmases spent baking in the kitchen with Mrs Gibbon, singing carols along to the wireless with her brother, taking long walks in the countryside in the brisk air with her father. She could shake all of these images and watch the snow fall around them the way the icing sugar used to fall through a sieve to top a Victoria sponge, each one like a scene from the handmade Christmas cards which her mother would send to cousins and aunts and uncles whom she had never met. The mirage of a perfect Christmas.

They spent the afternoon in the sitting room, listening to the wireless, watching out of the window as the snow fell thicker, listening to the carols. A radio play aired, a tale of goblins who hijacked St. Nicholas' grotto and forced the elves to make monstrous toys to be delivered to the world's children on Christmas Eve and trap them all in a time loop, so that Christmas morning would never again dawn. Darkness fell slowly from mid-afternoon, the white haze growing thicker. The snow was sticking and getting deeper before they finally heard the clattering of the front door.

A flurry of snow preceded their father into the hallway.

"Maud and her brood assured me they were leaving promptly as I left. She said we shouldn't wait for her to serve dinner."

"Hugo, that simply won't do. They are our guests; I should not be seen to be ungracious enough to sit down to dinner prior to their arriving."

"Very well, Carolyn, we shall await their arrival."

Ellie listened to this exchange as she watched the snow begin to pile in the driveway. Her aunt Maud, Maud's husband Gregory, and her cousins, Jack and John, would likely struggle to reach them. It would be a shame. They visited every Christmas. The boys, aged nine and ten, were like brothers to Eustace, her own nine-year-old brother. When it snowed, she and her father would help the three boys build a snowman while her mother assisted Mrs Gibbon in preparing the luncheon.

"Eleanor, perhaps you and your brother should help your mother prepare the dining room and then get yourselves ready for dinner."

"Yes, Father." She switched off the wireless and beckoned to her brother.

After laying the table for eight, Ellie filled herself a bath, enjoying the hot water enveloping her body whilst listening to the wind howling outside, rattling the window pane, whipping the snow into a blizzard.

Washing and drying herself, she pulled her clothes tight around her to block out the chill, filling

166

the bath again and calling out to her brother that his bath was ready as she passed his bedroom on the landing. She sat on her bed and watched the snow for a while, the trees shrouded in white, branches reaching out like claws in the darkened evening.

She changed into her eveningwear, her garments finished with a winter gown featuring a fitted corset and dresses flowing to the floor. Her brother knocked on the door, asking her to secure his bow tie for him, a skill he'd not yet mastered.

They returned to the sitting room, where they found their parents also dressed in preparation for dinner. They settled to await the rest of the family's arrival, listening to the wireless forecast the most severe snowfall in several years, recommending they do not venture out of their homes unless in the most necessary circumstances.

'In other news, authorities are seeking a man who absconded from prison earlier today. Edward Hitchfield, 42, who was convicted of two murders in March this year, escaped prison officials early this morning after being admitted to hospital following a minor injury. He has been described as medium-build, bearded, with dark hair but balding, last seen wearing prison-issue garments. Police have advised the public to be vigilant. They suspect he will have made changes to his appearance and urge the public to report any suspicions they may have.

'Elsewhere…'

"My sympathies are with anyone who is without shelter in this weather, whomever they be," Carolyn commented.

"This fellow won't get far in this weather," Hugo added. Ellie wondered fleetingly if it was truly their minds he was attempting to put at ease. "They'll have caught him in no time at all."

"Assuming he doesn't freeze to death," Ellie added aloud, looking out into the ever-falling snow. It sounded more savage to the ears than she intended. Neither of her parents commented.

They were silent as the news programme was succeeded by carols, the lyrics of *God Rest Ye Merry Gentleman* swelling to fill the room. They all gazed thoughtfully through the window into the ghostly glow of the dark night. No one broke the silence. Satan's power seemed particularly potent at that moment, with a man led astray somewhere out there in the wilderness, cloven hooves treading in his shadow.

A loud knock roused them from their rumination.

"Finally!" Hugo exclaimed, rising to his feet. He walked into the hall, Ellie following at a distance to help collect coats. Her father opened the front door.

Ellie hung back in the sitting room doorway as she saw beyond her father that it was not Aunt Maud and her family who had knocked their door. Outside stood a tall man, shrouded in the darkness of the porch, snowflakes covering the back of his long, black coat as he faced the blizzard. He turned, removing his top hat, bowing his head slightly.

"Good evening." He smiled, cracking the dark look that coloured his countenance. "Forgive me my intrusion. I am travelling into the village and my carriage has caught in a snow drift. May I trouble you for assistance in digging me out?"

Her father's answer was not immediate, Ellie supposing him to be as surprised as she was.

"Certainly," he said, recovering his composure. "My groundsman, Gibbon, will happily assist also. But there must be no talk of you continuing on your journey in this weather. Your horses can accompany my own in the stables and you must join us for dinner."

"That is most kind, but I do not wish to impose on you any more than is necessary."

"It is no imposition. We are awaiting my sister and her family, and Gibbon's wife always prepares more than enough food." He turned, seeing Ellie standing in the doorway, half-shielded by the architrave. "Lay another place for the gentleman, Eleanor."

"Yes, Father."

Hugo pulled the front door closed behind him as he ventured into the storm with the stranger. The grandfather clock ticked steadily in the vacated hallway. Ellie did as she was bade. It was some time before the men returned, in a sudden flurry of snow blown into the hallway, accompanied by much boot stamping.

"Look who we found getting themselves trapped in the very same snowdrift as the Judge here," Hugo boomed. The group crowded in behind him.

"…I find it a much more agreeable form of travel than the motor car…" The stranger's words were all but drowned out entirely.

Eustace ran to greet his cousins as Maud and Gregory each kissed Carolyn and Ellie in greeting. Their visitor hung back from the crowd.

"How remiss of me," Hugo said. "Judge Bernstein, my wife Carolyn and my daughter, Eleanor."

"My pleasure, Madam, Miss Eleanor."

Ellie smiled politely as he removed his hat and bent over her hand. His gloved fingers were cold, their grip on hers firm. She thought he was going to kiss her hand and felt her cheeks flush with embarrassment. Girls at school she heard often talk of their encounters with men, but her own knowledge of men was scant beyond those of her family and the masters at school. She believed little of what those girls said. As he raised his head away from her hand, she got a close look at his dark eyes, the minor strands of grey speckling his dark hair at the temples.

Dinner was a merry affair. Her father carved the turkey that filled the centre of the table, after politely enquiring of the Judge if he wished to do the honours. Their visitor declined, not wishing to deprive his host of a task he evidently relished. Maud quipped that, without his turkey carving, Hugo would have little to boast of for the next year, which was met with more raucous laughter from the adults, for whom the wine was flowing freely.

The three boys largely ignored the adult nonsense, taking advantage of their parents' focus on the stranger. The five adults talked and drank and laughed. There were many compliments for Mrs Gibbon's culinary prowess. Ellie listened, often laughing in the right places, attentive to the stranger's tales of his career as a Circuit Judge and Justice of Assize, though, in the company of the boys, he restricted his detailed tales to cases heard in the quarter sessions of his youth.

Bed for the boys followed shortly after dinner, due to the late hour at which they ate. Barely able to contain their excitement at the impending visitation, it took quite some time for them to settle. Ellie remembered when she had been little more than their age and they barely more than babies, when she read to them earlier in the evening before she also went to bed, gazing out to the stars hoping for a glimpse of the reindeer pulling the sleigh through the night. On more than one occasion, she had caught the glimpse of a light in the corner of her eye, convinced it shone from the front of the herd.

With the boys settled, she and the adults retired to the sitting room, her mother offering either port or sherry. Her father and Gregory went out into the grounds, returning shortly carrying a large fir tree between them, which had been stored in the stable after being felled, away from the prying eyes of the children.

"You can barely see your own hand in front of your face out there," Gregory said, breathless under the strain of exertion. Both men and the tree were covered in snow. "It's a jolly good job you arrived here when you did, Judge."

"Yes," the Judge said thoughtfully. "I am much obliged to you, Hugo, and your dear wife, Carolyn. I should have been lost to this storm were it not for your hospitality."

"We'll hear no more of it," Carolyn replied. "You are welcome to remain with us for luncheon tomorrow."

Ellie listened to this exchange, the Judge now thanking her parents once more, as she sipped her small glass of sherry. She disliked the taste, wishing instead for the port that had been served to the three men.

She, her mother, and Aunt Maud, began to decorate the tree once it had been erected in front of the window. Her father set about adding more wood to the fire, while she secured small candles, bows and trinkets to the branches of the tree. The snow still fell beyond it, now piled against the window where the wind had blown it. The conversation soon turned to the man who had escaped prison.

"I'd be interested to hear your thoughts, Judge," her father queried. "With it being in your line of work, this business."

"Ah, yes," the Judge said. "Edward Hitchfield. I heard his case. Cut and dried. He murdered his wife and daughter, buried their bodies in the garden."

"How awful." Maud shivered.

"It seems he picked the wrong night to make his escape," Hugo added, a return to his earlier reassurances.

"Quite," the Judge concurred. "He shan't have made it far in this weather. It would be a miracle were he to even survive."

"Does the Devil not protect his foot soldiers?" Ellie asked, using a long candle to light the small ones on the tree branches.

"Ellie, we do not speak of the Fallen One in this house," her mother muttered, as if their guest may not have heard any of what was said.

"Fear not, Miss Eleanor," the Judge said, perhaps having not heard Carolyn's words. "Christ protects His soldiers too."

With the tree decorated, the evening wound down. More drinks were poured, though Ellie had not finished her first. She listened to the adults talking until her eyelids began to droop. She excused herself and retired to her bedroom, where she changed into her nightclothes and drew the curtains around her bed. She had forgotten to ask her father to make up the fire in her room, feeling cold as she hugged the bedclothes around her slight frame. Exhausted from the day's activities, she soon fell into a heavy, dreamless slumber.

She awoke abruptly in the small hours of the morning, looking around at the dark shapes of the curtains drawn around her bed, caught in the moment where your brain is catching up with your conscious body. Something had definitely disturbed her. She sat up, unable to settle back to sleep. She slipped her feet into her slippers, which were under the bed, and pulled her dressing gown tight around her.

She inched open her bedroom door and looked down the landing. Silence reigned all through the house. There were none of the accompanying sounds to movement, but she remained convinced that something had roused her. Leaving her room, she approached the window, looking out into the night, seeking the source of her disturbance. It had stopped snowing. The night was still and silent, no signs of tracks in the unblemished snow. She leaned on the sill, her breath clouding the glass.

Surmising that one of the boys must have awoken, she first checked Eustace's room and the room next to it where her cousins were sleeping, opening each door a crack to listen into the darkness beyond. No sound of movement in either room. Knowing she could not settle back in her bed, she went downstairs, careful to avoid treading on the creaking boards too heavily.

The silence felt deeper on the ground floor. The sitting room was empty, candles extinguished and glasses cleared away. The ghostly reflection of moonlight off the snow gave the room an icy visage, devoid of the warmth and rich pallet of colour present only hours before.

A footstep resounded behind her.

She shrieked, turning, arms pinning around her and holding her mid-turn, a hand clamping over her mouth.

"Please. Don't be frightened, I'm not here to hurt you." The voice was thick with gravel, as if it hadn't been used in a long time.

She struggled to free herself, but the man held her too tight, his arm locked around her small frame.

"I'm here for your father, he owes me his life. That's all I want, no one else."

Ellie continued to struggle, trying desperately to open her mouth, squealing under his hand, cold and earthy against her face.

"Let me go to him and no one need get hurt."

Gaining some leverage under his sweaty palm, she was able to open her mouth and bite down on skin. Instinctively, he pulled his hand away. Ellie screamed. Taking advantage of his surprise, she ducked forward, tipping him off balance and loosening his hold on her torso. She screamed again as she hurtled forward on to the floor.

Panicked, the man fled past her, pushing open the front door and running out, slipping on the snow-covered driveway. She ran in his path to the doorway, looking out at the disturbed snow, deep footprints visible until she could see no further. She shut the door, locking and bolting it, breathing hard as the shock hit her, tears springing in her eyes.

Turning, she found herself face to face with the Judge. She gasped; so stealthy must have been his approach.

"I see you have become acquainted with our escaped convict." He smiled, a crooked distortion of his face. She couldn't see the glint in his eyes, but she was sure it was there.

"Please help me, Judge, sir. He told me he was here for Father, that Father owes him. What does he mean? Does he mean him harm?"

"He means to kill him, my child. He has lost his own life, very nearly. When I passed sentence, his sentence was death. His execution was to have taken place today. In the face of the noose, this is his final desperate act: he wishes to trade his life for your father's."

"Surely if he harms Father, it shall only be another crime for which he will be put to death?"

"The universe operates on balance. Light and dark. Life and death. Good and evil. Many years ago, a pact was entered into, a sacrifice of the balance of one person's life against another's. For one man to prosper, another must suffer. Or so our friend believes. He wishes to redress that balance in his favour."

"Can you help my father? Please. I shall be forever in your debt."

"There is, perhaps, a solution. But such a solution will require a sacrifice in order to tip the balance, a pact between you and I, a payment of such a debt. Are you willing to submit?"

"Yes, sir, anything. Please."

"Then consider this matter resolved. In exchange for such a resolution, you are required only a small sacrifice – with me, share all the first experiences of your life, from this moment on until the time of your death, at which time, you will have fulfilled the terms of our contract."

"I'm not sure that I understand, sir?"

"We make such an event of first experiences. I find often that first experiences are given unwarranted weight. Take, for example, first love. How such emotion drives us to distraction, monopolises our every moment, both waking and sleeping. How it tortures as we endure it and how it pains when it escapes us. Yet as we mature, our emotions and our passions become more stable, more reliable, more satisfying. How much better to be one's last love than one's first?"

Ellie stared at him as he spoke, trying to make sense of his words. Her heart had not yet calmed.

"Ah, but you do not yet know of such things, my child." He took the final step to close the gap between them, taking her hand in his.

She was aware of the door at her back, her bosom heaving against his chest. Here she was, alone with a gentleman, wearing only her nightdress, the tears not yet dry on her face. She ought to feel shame. She felt hemmed in as he brought her fingers to his lips, grazing them gently.

He leant forward and kissed her mouth. Her lips came alive, heat rising in them and pushing out the cold. She felt sensation stirring inside her. She ought to feel revulsion as his tongue became a carnal serpent of temptation against her own. As he took a step back from her, she gingerly touched her fingers to her lips. This first kiss, her first kiss, had put the seal on their pact.

"Now, go," he commanded. Unsure how she should bid him farewell, she uncurled herself from the doorway, looking to him for guidance and finding none. Without a cue to anything different, she lightly ran up the stairs. No more words passed between them. He remained quilted in shadow below.

On her way across the landing, she paused and turned back. She looked through the window and saw the Judge standing out in the snow. She watched him for some minutes as he stood, apparently in waiting.

Presently, he turned around to face the front of the house. She could see someone approaching, stifling a cry as she saw that it must be the man who had attacked her, covered in dirt and snow, his face mostly covered in a dark beard. The two men spoke for some time, before the escaped prisoner turned to walk away.

She stifled a cry, part astonishment, part anguish. The Judge was letting the prisoner escape. They had been accomplices all along, conspiring to corrupt her and murder her father. Fresh tears flowed. She realised the Judge had liked her tears, had surely been able to taste them on her lips.

The Judge reached into his coat pocket, calling out to Edward Hitchfield as he retreated. As Hitchfield turned, the Judge pulled out a pistol and shot him in the head. The body collapsed in the snow as the shot rang out like an explosion breaking the night quiet, red spattering across white.

Ellie ducked out of view, clutching a hand over her mouth, digging her nails into her face. Her breath rasped and her chest heaved, silent tears squeezing from her eyelids, warm on her fingers. She waited for her family to come spilling into the landing from their rooms, disturbed by the gunshot. But none of them came. No sound of stirring or voices questioning what they'd heard.

Shaking violently, Ellie crawled on to all fours from her crouch under the window, too terrified to look outside, scuttling to her room. She bolted the door behind her. She ran for her bed, pulling the curtains closed and the bedcovers over her head. Her entire body was covered in sweat, cotton glued to skin, yet she felt cold to her bones, shivering, her skin clammy.

She waited, her eyelids squeezed shut, ears hyper-alert to every sound. The clock downstairs chimed. She waited, hardly daring to breathe. The clock chimed again.

It was still dark when she heard hurried footsteps and the door to her room burst open.

"Merry Christmas!"

The three boys dived through the curtains surrounding her bed, falling in a heap on top of her. In spite of her anxieties, she hugged them all to her, maybe a little harder than usual.

"You ought to all go back to your rooms."

"Whatever for?" Eustace demanded.

"To get yourselves dressed, of course!" she replied, sitting up in bed.

"Oh! If we must!" Her brother sighed. "See you at breakfast."

Ellie changed as hurriedly as she could. She heard activity in the rooms below, as Mrs Gibbon prepared a festive breakfast for the family. She paused at the door. How should she behave with the Judge over breakfast? She felt herself incapable of the required deception of her parents.

She exited on to the landing, rushing to the window to look out on to the snow-covered ground. Where Edward Hitchfield had lain only hours before was nothing. Not even a trace of bloodied snow.

She walked downstairs into the hallway, seeing her mother in the sitting room, standing by the fireplace. Brightly-coloured boxes lay beneath the tree, labelled with names hanging from glossy ribbon. Her father burst in through the front door.

"Damnedest thing!"

"What is it, Hugo?" Her mother rushed to the doorway.

"The Judge's horses are no longer in the stable."

"I think our guest may have also departed." Carolyn handed Hugo an envelope, which he slit open.

"My dear sir," he read aloud. "May I pass on my most sincere gratitude to you and your lady wife for your kind and generous hospitality in my hour of need. I must continue on my journey and trust you will not be alarmed to discover my departure. I hope for the opportunity to reacquaint myself with you and your charming family in the future. Please pass on my warmest regards and best wishes for the season. Yours gratefully, Honourable Justice Burnstein." He folded the letter back into its envelope. "Good heavens. I shouldn't doubt that we shall never lay eyes on the fellow again."

Listening in silence, Ellie could think only of a pact, sealed with a kiss in the small hours of Christmas morning.

She heard the motor engine before she saw the car, trundling around the corner and coming to a stop outside their home, tyres crunching on the cobbles.

"Come on, Peter, it's time to go."

The five-year-old rubbed his eyes, fatigue denting his hitherto boundless excitement. She bundled him into his coat as Paul entered the room, full of apologies.

"I wasn't certain until the last moment I would be allowed use of the car."

"It doesn't matter, we can be on our way now."

The snow continued to fall as they made their journey. They bounced over gravel, cobbles and uneven dirt tracks, made worse thanks to a damaged tyre. The bitter chill cut down to their bones as they trundled along. She imagined theirs to be much like the journey the Judge had taken on the night they first met, his in a carriage pulled by horses rather than driven by her husband beside her.

She spent the year following that first visit on a precipice, flinching at the slightest sound as soon as she found herself alone or once darkness had fallen. Only then did she understand how her parents had protected and sheltered her from the world; never before had she felt anything like the grip that fear bestows over one's life. She became incredibly withdrawn, lost far too much weight, and lost interest in many things which had previously delighted or intrigued her young mind. As the year drew to a close, she found that he made good his promise. For him, she had held her first true fears.

On Christmas Eve, she travelled into the village to make the final payment on gifts for her family. It was there that she met him once again. He insisted on them dining together; there she found her fear mixed with a strange sort of pleasure. For twelve months, she had dreaded the moment he would kiss her again, but when he did, he left her with a longing she could not decipher, which cut deep into her. At seventeen, he was all she knew. In spite of herself, she was left with a deep sense of his absence and a desire to be held in his arms.

His words had proved prophetic; following her first true sense of terror, he had introduced her to her first experience of love. She waited a further twelve months until the moment she would see him again, a year fraught with unbridled longing and anguish. When the time arrived, he did not. She waited all day and late into the night, accepting early on Christmas morning that she would receive no visitor. Thus, her longing was succeeded by heartbreak.

What followed was a difficult transition. A death in the family of the postmaster, for whom she had worked since departing school, resulted in the sale of his home and his resignation. She worked for a time for the landlady at the village public house, before being rehired by the new postmaster. There were times when she wondered if her good fortune was influenced by someone unseen.

But with change came the realisation that everything could be left behind, including fear and pain. The clarity of hindsight told her that the Judge was no great loss; in fact, his absence proved to be a relief and a blessing. He represented the monster under her bed, the big bad wolf stalking the forest, the older gentleman who stole her heart because it felt obligatory that she should give it.

However, when she met Paul, she became convinced that the Judge was observing her from afar and had been for some time. For what he was awaiting, she could not know, but it tainted her newfound happiness with bitter sourness. The more her feelings for Paul developed, her paranoia increased exponentially.

Shortly after Paul had requested permission from her father for her hand in marriage, she came face to face with the Judge early on Christmas Eve as she crunched through the brittle early-morning frost. With a crooked smile and glinting eye, he reminded her of her promise to him and she realised the full extent of their pact. By promising herself to him, she was betrothed to him first and he had no intention of releasing her from his power.

He came for her after darkness fell, while her parents believed her to have retired early in preparation for her marriage to Paul the following morning. They waited in silence, standing beneath a street lamp on the road that stretched into the dark in either direction.

The whip cracked through the quiet of the night, wheels rattling as the carriage was pulled around a corner by two sleek black horses, both seeming deeply displeased to be here. They came to a halt beneath the street lamp, shaking their manes and stamping their hooves, grunting in displeasure at the thickening snow. She looked into their eyes and thought she could see her own terror reflected in them. A man jumped from the carriage, opening the door in the side for them. It wasn't only the cold that caused her body to shake violently as the Judge held her arm and led her to the carriage, lit inside by a small lantern.

As they commenced their journey, the snow fell more heavily, the horses growing evermore grumpy, snorting as if in derision at the humans' desire to travel in such conditions. Pulled through the night at speed, she was unable to follow their journey with her eyes, and soon lost track of how long they had been travelling.

When they came to a stop, they alighted in front of a large house, entirely unlit. A gaunt, elderly man greeted them before the front door. The snow had stopped falling and it was a clear night. She could see the red lining of the man's black hooded robe.

The inside of the house was heady with incense. A woman, also in a black, red-lined hooded robe, led her to a room where she was to be prepared. Ordered to remove her clothing and lie on a table in the centre of the small space, she was compliant as the woman rubbed a warm, oily substance into her skin. Heat pulsed from every pore in spite of the cold air. She stared at the ceiling high above her, trying to block out the sensation of the fingers hard against her skin.

The woman worked quickly. Once her entire body was covered, an amulet was hung around her neck, its weight immediate. Hanging from a thick chain, the amulet was circular, a five-pointed star within it, styled in the image of a goat-like head. Two rubies at its centre, the creature's eyes, reflected the candlelight, while at each point of the star was a skull, delicately crafted in silver, each with their own ruby eyes, smaller than those of the goat-like creature. The black metal was cold against her fiery skin, her heart thudding behind it. She was handed her own black hooded robe, lined red inside, gratefully drawing it around her body to cover her nakedness. The material clung to her oiled skin. She felt a little dizzy.

She was led to a larger room, where the gaunt man stood behind a large rectangular altar, covered in a red tapestry adorned with strange symbols she did not recognise. Three black candles were lit at both ends, whilst in the centre glowed a large, red candle. A coil of red rope was laid around the candle. To one side stood a silver chalice, to the other lay a silver-handled dagger. Both featured the same goat-like image that hung around her neck. She couldn't stop shaking, feeling the evil so close to her thudding heart. With his glowing ruby eyes, the Devil could see right inside her.

She flinched as a hand grasped her arm. Looking to her right, she saw that it was the Judge who held her. He was also adorned in a hooded robe. He eased her forward. They entered a circle on the ground, lined around the edge with salt. Again, within this circle was a five-pointed star. There were candles on the ground at each of its points, red like the one at the centre of the altar. A hand belonging to another robed figure closed the circle of salt and lit the candles. She and the Judge waited before the altar.

Standing behind it, the man with the gaunt face raised his hood over his head. A bell sounded, echoing around the room. Ellie realised that it was he who was ringing it, holding it high. It rang out three times, the seconds between each stretching out, the air charged with the vibration of the chimes.

"In Nomine Dei Nostri Satanas Luciferi Excelsi." The gaunt man's voice was as sharp as the bell. A chorus of voices repeated his words from around them. She gripped her hands together, still feeling dizzy. The incense was stronger in here.

"In the name of Satan, I call upon the forces of Darkness and the infernal powers within." More murmuring beyond the candles. "Today, we bear witness to the binding together of two souls in the Kingdom of Satan. I beckon the gods to join us and bestow their favour on this union, as we invoke their infernal address."

Ellie's head was beginning to spin, her eyes stinging. The mutter of voices repeated the man's words, a dutiful congregation. The words were repeating in her head like a mantra. Some names meant little to her, others she recognised, her dread growing deeper – Astaroth; Beelzebub; Lilith.

The diabolical priest, for that was demonstrably what he was, walked from behind the altar, moving anti-clockwise around the circle, swinging a censer rhythmically back and forth. The incense burned in emissions of red smoke.

"We solicit thee, Lord Satan, for you bringeth thine element of fire. May you ignite passion and fill them with all-consuming lust." The priest bowed, moving from the spot. Ellie could see a figure beyond the candle at the point of the star, the flame dancing on the robe. She saw the glint of eyes, a grip so cold clutching down on her heart that she thought it may stop beating in her chest.

"We solicit thee, Lord Lucifer, for you bringeth thine element of air. May you grant knowledge and wisdom, so they may share consciousness and vision." He bowed again, moving on, now directly behind them so Ellie could see nothing of his movement unless she turned around. The Judge's hand still held her arm.

"We solicit thee, Lord Belial, for you bringeth thine element of earth. May you grant strength and stability, so they may build a robust foundation upon which to flourish and set forth on the dark Lord's path."

Now back into focus to their right, the priest spoke into the blackness beyond the flickering candle once more.

"We solicit thee, Lord Leviathan, for you bringeth thine element of water. May you divine a desire for fulfilment of all the dark Lord's earth has to offer and allow them ambition as deep as the ocean."

He returned to stand behind the altar. Ellie glanced left and right, figures standing unmoving outside the circle. She was convinced the light caught a glimpse of eyes glowing as red as the rubies on the amulet.

"All who bear witness, lurking in the cloaking of darkness, hear me. Bestow upon our couple a bastion of solace and protection and bear witness to their union, so that they may go forth into the world under the protection of your divine darkness and submit to your dark will.

"Bride and bridegroom, from this moment your lives become joined." He circled the altar, taking

Ellie's hand and tying it to the Judge's with the red rope.

He looked at Ellie, handing her the chalice. "To this union, you bringeth the boundless, insatiable energy of Babylon."

He turned to the Judge, handing him the dagger. "To this union, you bringeth the expansive, dominating energy of Satan."

The Judge raised the dagger and she remembered the night he had raised a gun and aimed it at a man's head. In that moment, she thought he was going to murder her as he had him. But he sliced the blade across both of their joined hands, blood spurting from the wounds and running between their fingers, dripping into the chalice in her hand. It spilled over the edges and ran through her fingers. He pulled her hand closer to collect more of it.

"Babylon and Satan, woman and man, darkness and light," the priest chanted, joined in a chorus by the congregation, repeating, getting louder with each repetition. "Without the other, neither holds meaning. The universe is so birthed from the seed of their eternal war."

There was more murmuring from the unseen congregation, cries of "Hail, Satan!" from the depths of darkness beyond them. Ellie was asked questions and she answered them as bade, then the same was asked of the Judge.

The chalice was taken from her and, with it, the priest circled them again, seeking a blessing from each point of the star. Ellie's hand throbbed, while the incense stung her eyes. Returning to the altar, on their side, his back to them, the priest lifted the red candle and poured wax into the chalice, then turned and lifted it to Ellie's lips. The liquid was warm and metallic. She felt a drop dribble down her chin from her parted lips. The Judge also drank, spilling none. The chalice was set back on the altar.

"Have no fear, for Satan walks with you for now and for always." With the dagger, the priest cut the outer bonds of the rope, preserving the inner loop that secured the bloody hands. They pulled their fingers from it. The priest dropped it into the chalice with the remains of blood and wax, a flame igniting from within. "The Lord of Darkness has spoken of his approval. I now pronounce you man and wife."

The Judge kissed her; their mouths wet with blood.

There was much celebration in the hours that followed. Wine flowed and fires burned. Ellie's body felt numb and her head thick with wine and incense. To much chanting, she and the Judge jumped over broomsticks and disappeared through the flames, leaving the congregation to their merriment and debauchery.

Ellie woke in her own bed, unable to recall how she had reached there. Her head ached and her body was sore. She prepared herself a hot bath. She winced as she sank into the water. Lying there, she allowed the tears to fall silently. She cried still when her mother found her some time later. She believed her daughter overemotional ahead of her marriage to Paul and chose not to comment. Instead, she assisted her out of the bath.

"Oh, Ellie, you've cut yourself!"

Ellie looked down at her hand as a drop of fresh blood hit the surface of the bath water.

*

Light broke through the blizzard as the car slid the final few yards before finally coming to a halt. Carolyn was standing on the doorstep as Paul gathered Peter into his arms in the blankets they had wrapped around him. Eustace, now eighteen, took the keys to park the car out of the weather in the now unused stables.

Numb with cold and exhaustion, snow no longer melting as it collided with her skin, Ellie followed her mother into the source of light, Paul having already carried Peter in ahead of them.

"Take him through to the fire, Paul," Carolyn said. "You should all warm yourselves. There's food on the stove waiting."

"Can I go to him?" Ellie asked.

Her mother looked at her, the sadness palpable in every feature of her face. She seemed unsure of words, perhaps almost ready to insist she warm herself by the fire first. But the defeat formed in the line of her mouth and she nodded at her daughter.

The stairs creaked more each time she visited, like old and tired bones weary with the weight of the world. She knocked on her father's bedroom door and he bade her to enter. The hinges creaked louder too. The curtains on the right of the bed were drawn back, a chair at the bedside, from where her mother had been keeping vigil. Her father, propped up slightly with pillows, smiled when he saw her, a warm and full smile at odds with the frailty of his body.

"I wasn't sure if you were going to make it." The boom in his voice had faded.

"How are you, Father?"

"I've had better days, Eleanor. But haven't we all? How is Peter?"

"He is very well, Father, exhausted with excitement and the long journey."

"And Paul?"

"Very well."

"How about you, Eleanor?"

"I am well, Father."

"Yes, you have made something of your life. All your own doing, a family of which to be proud." He coughed uncomfortably. "There was a time I thought all that may be lost to you."

A shadow crossed Ellie's face. She feared he had known her secret all this time.

Her father sighed, sitting up higher on the pillows with some effort. "I've a confession to make. I have done many things of which I am not proud." He could see Ellie was making little sense of his words. "Edward Hitchfield has been visiting with me this evening."

Ellie went to great effort to disguise the shock that she was sure must have registered on her face. Mistaking her expression for confusion, her father sought to explain.

"You remember that Christmas Eve when the weather was much like this one? The night Judge Burnstein visited. Edward Hitchfield, the convict who had escaped prison, that we heard about on the wireless, he was on his way to find me. I do believe the Judge came to stop him."

"You knew the Judge?" Ellie struggled to restrain the abruptness in her voice.

"Yes." It came out in a strangled whisper. Ellie encouraged him to drink some water before he

190

continued. It was as much to allow her to regain her own composure.

"Before you were born, I knew Edward Hitchfield," her father continued. "We were young men together, striving to make our marks on the world. We were ambitious, but foolhardy with our money. One Christmas, after a few too many ales at the tavern, we first met the Judge. He offered us success, but at a cost. For success, we must sacrifice a family. We should never sporn children."

Ellie listened to the howling outside the window, the hammering of hundreds of spirits against the thin, cracked glass. She envisioned Edward Hitchfield lying in the snow, blood and brains spattered around his exploded skull.

"But success was not enough for me, Eleanor. I wanted it all, I wanted fortune and a family. Your mother, she so wanted children."

"I'm sure the Judge will have known that when he brokered his deal with both of you."

Her father said nothing for some moments, as if it were the first time he had contemplated that.

"I went to him," he continued, at length, "begged him to reconsider our deal. He relented, said there was a way I could have both, for there was a clause. Our deal had been for the success of us both, with a joint sacrifice. But the balance could be tipped in the favour of one man, if the other were burdened with the full sacrifice. I did not hesitate, selfish, despicable fool that I was. I sacrificed Edward without a second thought."

Her father no longer looked at her as he spoke. He stared at the curtains at the foot of his bed, saying no more.

"What did he want in return, Father?" Her voice remained calm and cool, a momentous act of control. He finally turned back to face her. She could see his shame.

"He wanted my first-born child."

She blinked rapidly, cold shooting down her spine. "And you agreed?"

"God forgive me, yes, I agreed, Eleanor. So foolish and selfish I was, I put my own desire for children above the children I did not yet have. He told me I could have many children, but all he wished for in return was the first. I acquiesced, a decision I have regretted each day since arriving at it."

Ellie watched the candle beside the bed flicker. She smelt the wax burning. She laced her fingers in her lap against the cold.

"When he arrived at our door that stormy Christmas Eve, I believed he had come to collect. I was powerless to prevent it. But Edward was also on his way to me, to avenge the life I had stolen from him, no doubt. In the end, he paid the price and freed you."

"What makes you believe that?"

Hugo was startled at the abruptness of her tone.

"Edward told me so himself. He explained he paid the price for you."

Ellie closed her eyes, fighting the image. She was unsure if her father had become delirious, for she knew it impossible that Edward Hitchfield could have visited with him this evening to have told him he paid the price for her. Though it was true, only not in the way her father believed.

"I was so grateful when I read the Judge's note that Christmas morning." The exhaustion lowered his voice, barely audible above the ongoing snowstorm. "You were free."

She could have wept then. So many years of pain had followed that encounter, but her father had not noticed. She could not take that from him now, couldn't reveal to him she had never been free of the man they called the Judge.

"Do you remember, when you were small, before your brother was born, how we would sing carols every Christmas Eve by the fire? I used to swing you, high above my head, thank the Lord for my beautiful little girl. They were the only moments I was truly able to forget his shadow hanging over us."

They were both silent for a long time. Soon, her father's breathing deepened and she left the room quietly. She joined her family downstairs, Peter now awake and begging to stay up to decorate the tree with the adults. The wireless was playing quietly, the faint notes of the carols drowned out by the chatter. Ellie stared out into the white wilderness; the snowflakes blown against the other side of the glass. She knew that, out there somewhere, the Devil still lurked.

Sometime later, her mother went to check on her father. His breathing had stopped, a look of peace finally fallen in his expression.

The snow had stopped falling, the wind had ceased, a silver glow breaking through the tree branches, reflecting off the brilliant white haze, the whole world throbbing in a bright glow.

Ellie sat in the sitting room, staring out of the window, listening to the peace and harmony. Soft footfall cracked it like an eggshell.

"I knew you would come."

"Thus, you waited."

Ellie stood and turned to the doorway. The Judge stepped into the light, his smile crooked under his hooked nose. He had barely aged a day, yet she could see the age in him now.

"You are not taking my son."

"Madam–"

"No." She refused to allow him to speak. "Our pact is no longer valid. I entered into it to save my father's life. My father is dead, you can no longer threaten me with it."

He remained motionless, saying nothing. His smile broadened.

"You are, of course, quite correct, Madam. Many would not have been quite so observant to the terms of our contract. I have contracted world leaders, none of whom have stumbled across the clause. For that alone, you shall hear no argument from me on the matter."

"So that draws a line under it. We shall part ways here, Judge. I am not my father or his associates. I do not desire wealth or power."

"You seem to have forgotten that was not the only pact into which we entered."

"You refer to our marriage in the eyes of Satan? I made vows before God, ones He knew to be the truth of my heart."

"You presume the benevolence and forgiveness of your God to not be equalled by the malevolence and vengefulness of mine?"

She could think of no response, but her legs suddenly felt weak.

"However," he continued. "It was not to our matrimony which I referred. I was referring to our pact of blood."

She felt the chill, remembering a cold so deathly, as he had lain her on the altar before which they had made their vows, pulled the cloak back from her naked body and consummated their marriage.

"I do not need to take your son, Madam. He is already mine. If you believed your husband's seed to be more potent than mine, then you were sadly mistaken."

She wanted to scream at him that he was wrong, yet she knew he was not. She had always known. She sank into the armchair.

"Merry Christmas, Madam, and good night. Until next year." He tipped his hat and turned and left the room, his shoes and stick clicking on the ground. Then he was gone.

Ellie stared out into the snow, at the trees beyond. Satan wasn't just out there in the darkness, lurking amongst the trees. He was inside our homes, hooves resting by the fire. He was inside us all, inside our children. Only time would tell if he could be defeated and cast down into Hell from the earth on which he roamed.

RUN

It is often the things we don't say which warrant the loudest voice. Sometimes the deepest silences ought to be broken, disturbed from beneath the headstones. That's easy for me to think now. It's easy to think of the things which you should have said, all of the things you wanted to say, those things you weren't brave enough to, when you're alone. In these lonely moments, I lie in the dark and listen to the rain pattering above, my eyes closed.

You followed me, didn't you? As you always follow me, day and night, from when I wake in the morning, through the lit hours of the day at a steady pace, a safe distance away, gaining on me as the dark yawned and stretched and slowly ate the light for its breakfast. When it has swallowed its last morsel, licking its lips with a glutton's satisfaction, I can feel you close, never quite sure how you managed to close the gap so quickly, reaching out a hand to touch my shoulder. It is then that I run, and you chase me through my dreams until morning, when we begin our *Danse Macabre* once again.

But I always knew the night would come when you would catch up with me.

It's difficult to pinpoint exactly where it began. Everything seems so jumbled, both of us so intertwined you could have been beside me on the day I was born. Of course, how could I remember if you were? Would you even remember?

When I try to look back, everything is so foggy. Strange, how our memory seems to develop at a slower rate than our brains do. As if they're separate, not truly connected at all. I suppose most people can only look back so far with clarity, back further still with less clarity, details beginning to merge or become clouded, further back again where entire events mould, parts of them confused, chunks missing or simply not true recollections.

I wonder, does the fog advance through your life as you do, some distance behind but a constant presence, clouding memories, leaving decay in its wake? In your early life, your childhood becomes lost and unclear, and your most cherished memories may not even be real. You reach the middle of your life and now your teenage years are lost too. How often parents appear to forget the past as their own children grow into them as teenagers. It used to amuse me. Now it only makes me feel sad. How much do we lose when we reach our later life? I don't think I'll get there to find out.

Is that when the fog starts to catch up with you?

I am in total blackness. Complete dark. I run my hands over the smooth wood of the wall beside me, conjuring images of my safe haven, a log cabin in the heart of the forest where you cannot reach me. A candle burns beside me. There is a small window above my head. I know you are outside, watching me through the glass, glimpsing my life but unable to reach me. I snuff out the flame, lying in the dark, listening to the rainfall; distant, unable to break through the thick canopy of trees.

*

197

Lying in bed, staring at the ceiling, I do not need to check the clock to know what time it is. You wake me at the same time every morning. I listen to the rain licking the window pane. Lights glow through the trickles, ebbing and flowing, reflections of yellow headlights and red taillights from the road. I feel the heaviness as you move, as if you have been slumbering beside me.

How long have we known each other, you and I? Some days, it feels as if you are a part of my every memory, a taint on old photographs, always there in my peripheral vision. But when did I really notice you, acknowledge you, recognise your presence? That I cannot truly recall.

There were nights when you held such power over me, crippling nights when I could feel your weight throughout my body, my brain on fire. You took a hold of me and I could not shake you off, a dark shadow latched to my back, hands wrapping around my throat, my head gripped within your claustrophobic embrace.

An endless cycle. I lie in bed, staring at the ceiling. The clock ticks on the bedside table. The seconds stretch out, widening, each gap seeming to grow longer, and yet at the same time I can feel my life slipping away at an alarming speed – empty, pointless, unfulfilled. Weeks, months, crammed into these stretched out and bulbous seconds, bloated and strained in twisted memories; your versions of them. How I long for the neat, rhythmic order of those seconds, ticking up to minutes and to hours. What a beautiful stretch of hours a day is, so full of possibility. Yet, with you as a companion, they are

198

frighteningly short, yet paradoxically endless within those bloated, ugly seconds.

Time. Remember how long a day would feel as a child; how only a few hours could feel like forever. How I long for that now. The clock speeds up as we grow older. There are times when I am visited by a recurring dream. I am on a cart; an old, wooden cart. Its sides feel like the walls of my cabin in the woods. As a baby, you are laid down in this cart and it sets off on its way. When I first experienced this dream, gentle arms bathed in light lay down these young souls. But I see the truth now. I see you. Darkness laid us down; sadistic glee made the cart begin to move.

The cart moves slow as it first begins its descent, but the speed increases steadily, then becomes too fast. We look back and wish we had more time to enjoy moments of that descent. Already, it is too late; we have missed so much more while we spent time looking back with regret. Turning, I see the end of the journey ahead, a huge wooden sign blocking the track. I am powerless to slow the cart, unable to prevent its crashing, crushing finality. There is only one spectator awaiting me. It is you, standing silent and in shadow. I can see your salivating mouth stretched into a grin.

I have so much that I want to do. The collision comes, bone and wood splintering, light waning and struggling. It extinguishes like a candle. All I can feel is you, clinging to me. You won't let me breathe and my chest is so heavy it feels like it will implode.

I sit up in bed, leaning over the side, trying to breathe normally, hearing my feeble attempts like an outsider. You place a cold hand on my shoulder. I shake you off. I do not want you. I never did. Selfishly, you chose me.

I leave my bed, tired of too often lying back and trying to sleep while those bulbous seconds fill to bursting. I am exhausted with the strain of it, of living with you. I go to the kitchen, running the tap and filling a glass of water. I try to stop my chest rising so sharply, wanting to be rid of the fluttering heaviness in my gut, like a nest of spiders. The water is harsh and jarring in my throat as I gulp it down.

There is movement in the shadows behind me. I cannot shake you away.

I dress quickly and leave the house. There is a light drizzle and I pull my collar tight around my neck. I have no hood and didn't think to bring an umbrella with me. I could turn back, but I need to keep moving forward. I don't want to turn back. I know you'll be there, my shadow.

I welcome the rain, welcome the cool drizzle hitting my face. It feels free, almost as if it can wash away all the heaviness that I carry each day. How I long for the freedom, the weightlessness that being free of you would mean. I can almost remember when you were smaller, practically a black speck I could brush from the corner of my eye. But you grew, feeding, a great weight around my shoulders. There are times when you don't feel so heavy; yet you remain, omnipresent. The rain makes me feel that it's possible you won't always be there.

I almost collide with another man on the pavement. He is soaked to the skin, hair unkempt and too long. I can see the delirium in his eyes. I wonder, is this how I appear to others?

200

"Why are people so cruel to each other?" he raves. Perhaps he talks to me, perhaps he isn't truly aware of my presence.

"I don't know," I reply weakly.

"How can people be so cruel to the homeless? We're human beings, we're the same as you." He stands apart, crying out to the world. He doesn't see me as human either.

"I'm sorry."

I move on, feeling useless, sorrow like an albatross on my heart.

Ahead of me, traffic lights blink green, but there is no traffic. Another walker, a sensible one, unlike me, with his hood up, waits to cross the road. I reach the gap in the fence and divert through it. I don't want to connect with other people, to be close to their noise. Far too much noise. It seems so loud when you are at your heaviest.

An abandoned newspaper, sodden and disintegrating, lies beside the fence. The headline is fading – POLICE HUNT KILLER OF LOST SOULS. Our world is cruel and deteriorating. I hardly recognise it anymore. But has it changed, or was it you or I that changed?

Trees close in around me. There is some shelter from the rainfall here. I slow my pace. In the dark, I have strayed from the path, feeling the weeds tangling around my ankles like tentacles. Branches claw at my wet hair, leaves slithering along my head.

Somewhere behind me, I hear rustling in the trees. I turn, searching the dark behind me. I am not the only one here.

Raindrops pierce the leaves, dripping down. One of the tree trunks moves, not a tree at all. I turn from it and run.

"I've been running for a very long time. There are times when I've run until I can no longer breathe, staggering, falling to my knees and dragging myself on. But I can never stop. It's been so long. There are times when all I want is to stop, and others when I can think of nothing worse. I don't know if that makes sense?"

My new friend sipped from his mug, a thoughtful expression creasing his face. "Yes, I think I understand."

I looked around at the empty booths alongside us, at the darkness through the windows beyond. We were tucked away from view, around the corner from the bar. I could see the rain falling under the streetlight through the window. I drank from my mug, enjoying the coffee's refreshing bitterness.

"Thank you," I said.

My breathing reduces to hard and shallow gasps, my chest rising quickly in an effort to meet my body's need. I lean against a tree trunk, looking back the way I had come, squinting in the dark, eyes darting across my field of vision. I see nothing. But I know you are there. You are always there.

"Please! Please will you just let me go."

I stumble on, physical movement the only fight I have against my mind's imprisonment, the chains you have wrapped so tightly around me. I strain against them, at times hearing the scraping of stone as the walls around me yield to the pressure. Ours is a constant war, the balance tipping back and forth. At times, the walls close around me, the chains constricting so tight I imagine they may snap my bones. There is never a victor. Or perhaps, if there is, it is always you.

The rain penetrates the leaves and branches, soaking me still. I close my eyes and turn my face up to it, feeling it splatter against my skin and run down my face like a veil of tears, the taste of it on my lips. I sigh, heavy, weighted with memory.

I remember the rain. I remember you. No…not you. I remember her.

I remember the rain. How it lashed down with ferocious rage. She was driving to meet me, but didn't know her way. I told her to stop where she was and walked to meet her, her headlights shining through the downpour from where she'd pulled over to wait at the side of the road. She laughed as I clambered into the car, soaked to the skin.

She had to park around the corner from my home as there were no spaces in my street. By the time we reached my front door, she was as drenched as I, water running in waterfalls down her face. We laughed as we rushed into the porch. She was worried her makeup had run. I told her that she was beautiful, with her delicately applied eyeliner now a cloud around her eye. Our eyes locked in that moment. A moment I wish could have gone on forever. Time stood still. She kissed the rainwater from my lips. We peeled off each other's sodden clothes and made love for the first time on the rug in front of the fire.

I can still feel the heat from the flames as we lay beside the fire in the afterglow. I ran my fingers up her spine and the tickles made her giggle.

I lean my head against the rough bark. There was something else, another feeling that moment brought me. I had felt alive, I had felt…free. You had gone.

"We became serious very quickly after that night. It had only been our third date, but there was just that magic between us, you know? I knew I loved her very soon afterwards, but I took my time to say it. Those words change everything, don't they?"

The man smiled in agreement.

"I'm sorry, here I am, burdening you with my life story. I'm not sure complete strangers should be expected to listen."

"Sometimes strangers are best. You don't have the burden of someone you know hearing your personal feelings."

I nodded. "The world is bigger than we know it to be, I suppose. We should help each other more, as a species I mean. There have been times, when the day is particularly dark or the strain has been particularly heavy, when it feels like a stranger has reached out a helping hand. Simple things, like striking up a conversation in a queue, or a smile or a greeting as they pass by. Not enough people do that. But, you know what, just with that simple acknowledgement, those people may have saved someone's life today."

I have strayed too far from the path, without hope of finding my way back to it. The trees loom before me from out of the darkness, trunks thick and stretching high into shadow, closing in on me from all directions. There is a tightness in my chest, a lightness of breath that I barely notice, so often it is my ailment. Shapes move in the corner of my eye, yet when I turn to look, no matter how hard I squint, I find no clarity. This forest has the power to make a stray cat look like a panther stalking between the trees.

Rainwater continues to break through and sting my eyes. I trip over thick roots and fallen branches, scraping my skin against bark and bracken.

I look around, change direction again, trying to find a clue that I am successfully heading back the way I came.

No matter my direction, at a distance, something follows. It is malignant. No longer am I sure that it is you. I quicken my pace. The wind whistles down through the leaves, manipulating the fall of water to bespatter my face. I dance around the branches, the thick looming trunks that crowd narrowly. It is becoming difficult to pass them.

The wind carries the voices to my ears, indistinct, at a distance. I try to ignore them. Yet they remain; the soft, throaty emissions, growing ever louder. The trees are giving voice to their howling. It becomes clearer, like a translation is taking place, carefully deciphering a foreign tongue just one letter at a time, unscrambling the static from a transmission until it is intelligible and distinct.

"Help us," they whisper. "Please help us."

"She had a beautiful little girl."

I felt my grief pour out of me, like a dam had finally broken, succumbing to the pressure that over years never abated. I'd reached across the void and connected to a stranger. He sat impassive opposite me, occasionally sipping from his drink – black tea to my espresso. For the first time, I wondered if he was a counsellor or therapist, so good he was at listening.

Little Rosie, as I'd called her when we first met, seeing her shy smile as she peeked at me from beneath her golden blond hair, tightly holding on to her mother's hand. She had her mother's wide hazel eyes, her little curls behind her ears. She adored me from our first meeting. She melted my heart.

She was so excited to see me every time I visited, eagerly telling me stories about the things she'd learnt in school that day, showing me her toys, asking questions; always asking questions.

Of course, at first I was simply known as her mother's friend, but she was no fool. At five years old, she already possessed the knowing grin which would spread across her face whenever there was talk of Mummy's friend. Her mother recounted a conversation they'd had one evening, very early in our relationship:

"Do you ever get lonely, Mummy?"

"Why would I get lonely, when I have you?"

"I know, but I mean…do you want someone special, for you?"

"They would have to be very special, special for both of us, Rosie."

Someone like me, then, Rosie had said, because she liked me.

Even now, that memory thaws my heart.

One evening, after I finished reading her a bedtime story, she promptly got out of bed and closed her bedroom door, rounding on me, her intelligent eyes gleaming behind her glasses.

"Are you Mummy's boyfriend?"

"You know you should probably ask her those questions first," I replied with a smile.

"You love her though, don't you?"

Though I'd not yet said the words, I knew they were true, and so did Rosie. I told her yes. I couldn't lie to this clever little girl with her knowing eyes and beautiful heart.

"She loves you too."

I listen to the whispers, growing louder and more urgent. I stumble, balancing my body against trees, squeezing my eyes shut, willing them to stop tormenting me with their agony. They turn the key on my vulnerability, opening the door for you. You no longer follow me. You possess me. I can feel you in the pit of my stomach, hollowing yourself a crevice in which to lurk, insidiously flooding my body with poison. You wrestle with my mind. You want my soul. I might just give it to you.

"Help us. Help us." Urgent, insistent. Pain jars in my ears, piercing my brain with red hot needles. Who are they, these emissaries of yours with the scalding voices?

I have spent far too many nights with you to not know the signature of your presence intimately. The cold shiver of your touch. The scent of your decay.

"Join us." The whispers reach out for me, beckoning me deeper into the forest. I should not go, but I am pulled deeper. Your voice joins them, wicked and cruel.

"You don't want to feel like this any longer. You'd be better off with them."

I press my hands against my ears, praying for all the noise to stop.

There were nights when I held her a little too tight. I was afraid. She enjoyed being my place of peace, where I could finally relax and be my true self, feel a sense of happiness and belonging. But did I hold too tight? When she was by my side, you were lost out in the dark. Yet still I feared you. I feared your return, your vengeance.

There was no noise in my head then. Only the tender breeze, the gentle waves, the birds singing. And her sweet voice. Like a lullaby, the lullaby she sang to Rosie as a baby. I wonder what Rosie would be like now. Does she still see the beauty in the world? Or does she know you?

You snarl in my ear.

"You have no place here." You must truly hate me. How can I blame you? I hate myself too.

Exhaustion pulls on my eyelids. If only I could stop. Perhaps I won't wake from it. I long to no longer hear your voice.

From the depths of the forest, a scream pierces the night.

Splinters tore into my skin, ripping my flesh as I hit out at the walls closing in on me in the dark like the tangle of trees.

"What are you running from?"

I cried out, my scream scratching my throat hoarse, despair finally overcoming me.

*

The area in which we sat was dark. I was unsure if the poor lighting was due to the early hour of the morning or if it was common practice. A canvas hung on the wall in the corner – trees rising high, dark greens and splashes of autumnal orange, a narrow brook snaking crookedly into the depths of the forest. I stared into their shadows. There you were, staring back at me. I blinked, held my eyes shut momentarily.

You had gone.

I averted my gaze, past the television silently playing the latest headlines, to another canvas – warm yellows and vibrant blues; a summer scene, a sandy beach beside the sea. It took me back to summers long gone by, running with Rosie in the sand, the three of us laughing in the waves. Long, hot days full of peace; cosy nights beside campfires in the sand. I knew a long time ago that I could never make memories like those again.

I wondered if she thought of me now. We all have cherished childhood memories; does she hold any of me, remember those same times I do? Or have memories of me been lost to the mists of time?

Did she think that I abandoned her when I didn't say goodbye?

I sipped my drink, mulling over my memories. He watched me, placid, making no movement that may implore me to speak if I did not wish to.

"One evening, after I had cooked her chosen meal and we sat down at the table to eat, she said it was like I was her dad."

"Can I call you Dad?" she asked.

"You have a dad," I pointed out, smiling. But my heart was glowing, so full of love for this child whom I wished was my own.

She shrugged. "I can have two. Other girls have two. And you're like a proper dad."

"Thank you. Maybe we should see how Mummy feels about it."

"It can be for when I'm with you. Our secret. Dad."

I watched my little girl eat her dinner. It felt the furthest away from you I had managed to reach in my entire life.

I should notice the signs, for I know them in refined detail. I know when you are nearing, when I am safely out of your reach and when you are closing in. Yet so often you are able to trick me, reaching out and taking hold so I struggle to shake free of you. I know the symptoms of your presence. When life becomes dog-eared and tainted, when the days seem a little too long, when even my soul feels tired. I ache to reach out in the middle of the night to hold someone, to talk, to connect. But there is no one there. Only you. You comfort me with your suffocating embrace, swallowing me with your blackness, shrinking my world to a pinprick so that light cannot get in.

"Are you there?" the trees whisper to me, mournful. "Can you hear me?" Desperate, longing for a hand to hold. "Help me." Your other victims, imagining me a hero, not the weakened wanderer as lost as they are.

"I'm here." My cry is lost amongst the leaves and the pattering rain, its downpour growing louder in response, mocking my attempts to reach out to someone in the dark.

"Where are you?" I try once more, but they are silent now. Perhaps they can hear in my voice how useless I will be to them, not the action hero of lore, just the sad worthlessness of reality.

I push on through wet leaves, branches jutting up to snare my ankles. My crashing and fumbling through the undergrowth is loud to my ears, merging with the growing wash of rain. There is faint rumbling at a distance. It may be the traffic on the road or carriages rattling along the train tracks, people beginning their days or heading home after a long night. They are so far away from me right now; I am outside of their lives. It makes me feel so crushingly alone.

I hear another sound beneath the rain. It strikes cold deep into my heart and trembling erupting throughout my body. Sobbing that wells up from the soul; wrenching emotion. It pierces the density of the trees, the solidity of the dark, the incessant hammer of the rain.

Unease ripples through me in spasms. Something burrows through your grip on my mind and tells me that I should not be here; it is not safe and I should leave immediately. There comes another mournful wail. I am rooted to the spot. The whispering has stopped, listening with me. I can barely breathe, my body straining and gasping for air. I do not know which way to turn.

There is another cry, this one subdued, the fight evaporating from them. I decide; I cannot leave another desperate soul to rot under your spell. I will find them and we will leave this place together.

My movements are quick and determined as I stomp through bushes and kick up leaves, pushing branches out of my way, twigs catching in my hair and scratching my face. They get more vicious, the whisperers jealous that I did not choose them to save.

I round a thick trunk and am kicked in the face, sending me sprawling back into nettles. I try to shake the confusion out of my head, but it sets in deeper. I look up, a man above me. He swings to the side, then back, gravity still pulling on his corpse, stretching his broken neck, purple and elongated, eyeballs bulging from their sockets. Another poor soul who fell victim to you, out here in the forest without hope.

I am a failure. The hanging man tells me that with his lifeless stare.

Dragging myself up, my mind feels far away as I continue, past the man and further on, my pace slackened. I am aware of my physical body's movements, but they feel laboured, my mind's awareness dimmed, as if observing from afar. I traverse thickets and step over large roots and fallen branches. My body is heavy and cumbersome. I look around as if trying to find something to cling to, to ground myself. My brain aches with strain and fatigue and the torment of a man who put a noose around his neck to escape you.

I hear crying again, quieter still, barely audible over the torrent of rain, that I am unsure if it is not my imagination. I find it harder and harder to breathe. Then I see her, sitting at the foot of a tree, a small girl. I approach her cautiously, unsure if she has seen me yet. I stoop down when I am a few metres away from her.

"Are you hurt?" I ask.

She does not answer, keeping her head bowed. She is trying hard to mask her crying; the short sharp breaths that rock her head and shoulders the only remaining sign. I try again.

"Do you need help?"

She raises her head a fraction, but her hair is hanging in her face and I cannot see her eyes.

"It's okay," I say. "I can help you."

She stifles her crying, raising her head a little further upwards.

I risk moving closer. Her head shoots back in alarm, her eyes wide and wild with panic. She jumps up to her feet and runs, crashing into the bushes and from my sight in seconds. I heave a deep sigh, her feral expression of terror cutting into me. She has learnt to fear men: either taught by a woman who learnt the lesson herself, or by a man who taught her the lesson first hand. Sorrow grips me. I cannot wish for it to be any other way while there are such men in the world. It will protect her. But it also means I cannot help her, another lost soul fallen prey to you.

The rain continues, relentless, and in it I can hear you laughing.

Memories flooded back. Comfortable evenings spent with an arm around each of my girls. Rediscovering old family films and introduced to new ones besides. Walks in the sunshine; a holiday in a caravan on the coast, when we lit a fire on the beach after watching the sun go down.

She and I, walking hand in hand; afternoons spent in the sun, hours spent talking and laughing. Long nights in each other's arms, philosophising on the mysteries of life; the arts of books and films and music. Decorating the house into the early hours of the morning, smudging paint on each other's faces and showering together when we should have been sleeping. Falling asleep together while talking on the phone on the nights when we were apart. She and Rosie had become the centre of my world.

Always, I remember the rain. Days and nights drenched by it. She looked so beautiful in the rain, her hair wet and droplets glistening on her cheeks. I used to kiss the raindrops from her face and taste them on her lips, peel her wet clothes from her body like we did on that very first night. Late nights spent making love and listening to the world outside, safe in each other's arms. I recall those nights when it rained the most.

Driving, driving through the rain, windscreen wipers rubbing against the windscreen with each swipe. Her eyes were closed, resting peacefully. The cats' eyes blinked at me as I passed them. I opened the window an inch for some fresh air. Rosie stirred behind me. I glanced in the rear-view mirror.

"Is Mummy asleep?"

"Yes."

"Are we nearly home, Dad?"

I smiled. "Almost there."

"Are you lying?" She laughed.

"Now you know I would never lie to you. I'd always get caught."

She giggled, watching the headlights of passing cars. I indicated to leave at the next junction.

214

"I love you, Dad."

A lonely tear trickled down my face.

"I often still hear those words, but then I look in the rear-view mirror to find she isn't there."

I stopped talking, looking down at the table for a moment that stretched. He didn't speak, waiting for me.

"I still miss them every day. Some days get harder to bear than others." I hesitated again. "Anyway, enough about me for the moment. How about you? Tell me your story."

"There's plenty of time for my story," my new friend replied. "You ought to finish yours first. I think it's important."

I didn't respond at first. He allowed a few more moments of silence, space to order my thoughts.

"I sense you're reaching the most painful part. You're trying to avoid it, to look away. Face it, you can do it."

I sighed, leaned back in my seat and ran a hand over my weary eyes. I needed so badly to sleep.

"You're right. This is the most difficult part."

It feels as if I have been wandering without aim for many hours, though I have no concept of time. I've not brought a watch or a mobile phone with me. I am hopelessly lost, another damned soul amongst all the others in this forest of forgotten voices.

The girl has vanished. At first I searched for her, but my hunt proved to be in vain. I look for a way out of the trees, but that also proves a feat too taxing for my mind.

By now, I am shivering violently; the cold rain has seeped through my clothes to my skin. I long for a hot shower and the warmth of my bed, to finally fall into a deep, restful sleep. Each night, no matter how exhausted I am, my mind does not rest, refusing to succumb. I cannot remember the last night I slept straight through until morning.

I stagger past a tree and realise I have arrived in a clearing hidden within the density of woodland. I'd not become aware that the rain had stopped, yet it must have done. Its sound had become a constant thrum in the background, yet all I can hear now is silence, as crystal clear as a bell.

Before me is a pool of water, its surface like a sheet of glass, undisturbed by rainfall. Cloud cover has dispersed a little, the reflection of stars giving the water the glow of black crystal.

I sink to my knees at the water's edge, mesmerised by its stillness. It looks back at me, imploring me with its depth. I close my heavy eyes, sharing my burden as it shares its own with me. We are comrades, both abandoned in the deepest recess of the forest. There is no sound here, none of the distant rumblings of life nor the closer calls of the night birds. No wildlife comes to this pool to drink. They sense its sorrow and keep their distance. I know how that feels. Far too many human beings are oblivious, while others keep that same safe distance from me, as if afraid they will be touched by the sorrow that you bring, to be sucked down into the depths by your pandemic of pain. I feel great affinity with this pool, we alone together in the dead of night.

Opening my eyes, I see something shimmer on the surface at the pool's centre. I cannot identify it. I stand and go to the water's edge, straining my eyes.

But I am not close enough, thinking it must be something reflecting the night sky on the surface of the water. I look down at my feet, my shoes already sodden through. I wade in up to my ankles, the smooth surface rippling as I push through. Weeds wrap around my feet, tugging me deeper.

Still struggling to identify what I can see, I wade further, the water heavy and resistant. A great heaviness pushes down on me, this clearing carrying a weight that chills me far more than the water that is seeping into my clothes. I am now in up to my waist, almost within reach of the centre. I stretch out my fingers, grasping them around human hair, which floats on the surface of the water.

I recoil in shock, the underwater plants tightening their grip on my legs as I move backwards. The shimmering object is a human head, now turning in my direction after I'd pulled on its hair, rising out of the water as it turned, its white shroud glued by the water to the skin beneath.

She turns fully to face me. I gaze into her face, the face that has haunted a thousand broken dreams, the face I have kissed a thousand times. Her eyes sing to me, a silent song of sorrow. All this time, I haven't seen your face. Of course, it would be her face; who else's face would you have?

I look at the lips I've craved to kiss every day since I lost her; the body, that I've ached for in the cold hours of the morning, beneath the clinging white shroud. Slowly, she raises her hand, fingers trembling, the water dripping from her fingertips. I look at her face, the torrents of water streaming from her hair like they did on that night all those years ago.

I lift my own trembling hand, realising we are slightly out of reach of each other. I stretch, my fingertips brushing the pads of hers.

A loud screech breaks the silence. I look up sharply as a large shadow swoops over my head, an owl daring to shatter the silence. I look around at the still pool, so unnatural here in the centre of the forest, where no life filters through and pain is master. I take a step back, branches twisting more tightly to hold my legs.

I turn my head to look for her and you lunge at me, her once beautiful face twisted into a hideous, malformed husk. A single eye swivels in its socket, the other socket gaping and dripping with puss. You open your mouth, maggots erupting with your roar. Her long hair is matted and strewn with knots around your shoulders.

Your splintering fingers close around my neck, pushing me down, the water sucking on my body like a vacuum opening up in the depths of quicksand. I can smell the stench of Hell on your breath as you hold me in your grasp. You have fine-tuned my torment for far too long for me to stand any chance of escape. You drag me beneath the surface and I await oblivion.

My lungs struggle to draw more breath, pulling in only water. Coherent thought is rapidly abandoning me. I think of the lost little girl. I hope she finds her way home. I am floating, drifting. But you can not resist a final cruelty, spitting me out and letting my lungs draw in a ragged, agonising breath. I splutter and spit water, my body clawing for life even as I no longer want it. Just let it be over.

218

But my body refuses to fight its desire to survive. Freed from my restraints, I clamber on to the muddy shore, looking back at the water, aggression rippling across its surface. I watch as it smooths over, returning to the burdened quiet.

You watch me with her face. You hold out the hand I held on so many nights, when I believed you were far away. I get to my feet and run.

Hindsight is a powerful vantage point. From its lofty position, you can interrogate, analyse, decipher and evaluate. Yet it renders you powerless. I've often punished myself for being so foolish as to not have known, screamed at my reflection's insufficiency, shouted abuse at the worthless fool that stared back at me with red-rimmed eyes, his heart full of sorrow, my own now full of rage.

I should have noticed the signs.

You had crept back into my life; slipped through the cracks one night while I slept. But it took me many days, perhaps weeks, to acknowledge you, by which time you had already taken your hold. At least, that's what I believed at the time. The truth was that you'd never fully relinquished your hold on me. You'd simply shed your skin, deceived me anew.

I ignored you at first, tried to continue with my normal life. The irony was that I dismissed the things that caused me alarm as symptoms of your insidious game. Only hindsight showed me their significance, how the days and weeks and months I fought my silent battle with you masked what was to come.

On the eve of my birthday, I was required to stay away from home while taking part in a training course for work. I felt tired that day, having slept little the night before while trying to keep up with everything circling around in my head. She had kissed me goodbye in the morning and told me not to worry. I spent most of the day wishing I could be with her, to find the peace she always instilled in me.

We spoke on the phone that evening after I'd arrived at my hotel room. It was also Rosie's evening at her grandmother's, so she told me she was going to visit a friend and promised to call me when she got home.

I felt too tired to socialise; instead, I ordered room service and tried to relax with a book.

I awoke at 2:00AM, as had become my customary time to wake, the lights still on, my book beside me. I checked my phone. I had no missed calls, no messages. Perhaps she hadn't wanted to wake me by the time she got home, or maybe she had simply forgotten her promise. But it gnawed at me and I slept fitfully for the remainder of the morning.

I woke late and so painfully in your grip that I could barely move. Panic set into my limbs, my breath rasping from my chest. There was no usual birthday message from her, no phone call to say she couldn't wait to see me later. Something was fundamentally wrong.

My body shook violently as I dragged myself from the bed. I realised how late it was: I had missed breakfast and would surely miss the train, but neither registered as significant. I felt nauseous.

Leaning over the basin in the bathroom, staring at the mirror on the wall, I stared into your dark eyes that stared at me from my own eye sockets. I felt your spindle-like fingers wrapped around my heart, crushing it. I felt I would snap from the inside out.

I fumbled with my phone, dropping it to the floor. Picking it up, I dialled her number, needing to hear her voice. But it went straight to voicemail. I felt ice cold, right through to the core. Images assaulted my mind, scenarios spinning webs and developing a life of their own, multiple versions of the future weaved from this single moment where time had frozen. My breathing became hoarser, the burden heavier. My head swam, making connections I did not want to make. Of all these horrific visions, one stood out for its simplicity and deductive reason. I was hit with brutal conviction. I vomited violently, my body heaving with crooked, wheezing breaths. I was unable to stand, gripping the edge of the toilet, pathetic. I knew that she had woken this morning in someone else's bed, was probably still with him now.

I should have noticed the signs. I should know them in refined detail by now.

Unable to travel back with my colleagues, I told them I would catch them up at a later connection. They were content to blame a hangover, apparently forgetting I had not spent the previous evening with them.

My journey home was troubled. I eventually received a lacklustre birthday message from her. I found myself telling her the story of my sickness, without the trigger behind my panic, praying I was suffering a delusion, that I would arrive home to find my paranoia had reached astronomical levels. It was one of the more intimate symptoms of your infection – learning our innermost fears and, with them, betraying us. Such suffocating thoughts, so often wrong, sometimes conspiring to create a self-fulfilling prophecy. But there are times when those thoughts are not unfounded, when they speak truth. In those moments, our worlds shatter.

Until the moment I put my key into the front door and pushed it open, my mind could function in a world where everything beyond the door was as it should be, defences resolutely built because my mind felt too fragile to cope with the alternative. You whispered in my ear, the devil on my shoulder, assaulting me with images of her with another man, of what life would be like without her and Rosie in it. Both realities fought for dominance over my mind until I stood in my porch and heard the silence of the house greeting me. No running feet, no warm welcome, no hugs and kisses. They had left me.

She told me that she needed some space, that she and Rosie were going to stay at her mother's for a few weeks while she worked things out in her head, that she wasn't sure what she wanted. Such weakness and lies. Yet I was foolish enough to ignore the permanence of her actions, to hold on to the hope that they would be coming home. When we met to talk, when she finally had the courtesy to share her decision with me, it was I alone who was the cause of the breakdown of our relationship; I was too intense and she felt smothered by my emotion. I was in shock. It was only afterwards I considered the retaliation that all of these traits that so smothered her were the very traits which had apparently attracted her to me in the beginning. My intensity, my emotion, my commitment, my desire for her. I could not understand, but she would not explain it to me. I was defeated and did not know how to argue. I had little choice in the matter; this was no negotiation or compromise. She had made the decision and I was powerless to prevent my life crumbling.

You watched me break. I needed her more than ever in your presence. I asked to see Rosie. She said it was probably best not to. I have always wondered what Rosie was told, if she believes I abandoned her when I had gone and never saw her again. Two hearts broke that day.

I blamed myself. Of course I did; what else was I to think? I wasn't good enough; I must have let her down. She claimed my actions had led her to this decision. As much as this made little sense to me, I had no other evidence with which to work.

In only a matter of weeks, I found out about her new partner. It broke the last part of me. Somewhere in my heart, I'd still hoped for a reconciliation. Her reluctance to be honest ripped me apart anew. The truth began trickling through. The suspicions; the true opinions that others had previously hidden from me; those that had seen them together or seen her somewhere unexpected – yet the timeline did not align. Reason broke through. You will allow its use when it fits perfectly with your plans. No one rips apart their life with one person and makes a life with another in such a short space of time without an element of crossover. Who would skip the flirtation, the burgeoning attraction, the seduction, dawning familiarity, the dance of courtship? There was no one better placed to know her moves as I, for we'd danced that song before. She would not neglect it.

She was not the person I fell in love with, that much was clear. The woman I loved was not dishonest, deceitful, selfish or uncaring. Where had the honest, truthful, selfless and kind woman vanished to? Perhaps she had never truly existed. Yet still I loved her, only now with a brittle, lonely desperation. But you were there, as you always had been, awaiting my hour of need. Under your mentoring, I learnt how to hate her. Meanwhile, you taught me I could never be enough for someone – if even she didn't want me, why should anyone else?

"My friends all said I was a fool to get involved with her, to commit to her and the responsibility of someone else's child. There were things right at the very beginning that should have raised alarm bells. What is it they say? Fool me once, shame on you; fool me twice, shame on me? They were right, I was a fool. No relationship is plain sailing, but, in hindsight, I allowed her too much space for her own broken heart, for her own dark days, but not allowing myself to care for my own. I allowed her a distance that was damaging at times, because I knew what it felt like to crave silence. She took advantage of that.

"I still see her sometimes. I don't know which are worse: the days she walks past me as if I'm not even there; or the days she engages with me as if nothing has happened. I think she genuinely believes that nothing did. She doesn't feel my pain. She never did. That probably hurts the most, knowing you were nothing to someone who was everything to you."

224

I fell silent, my story told. The man opposite me watched me intently, as if waiting for me to continue. For a while, I did not, instead listening to the gentle rhythm of early morning. Traffic was sparse. A train rattled by. No talking, no bustle, perhaps the tread of a single set of footsteps, splashing through the puddles the rain had left.

"I still experience irregular moments where her shadow crosses my memory. It's accompanied by the crushing realisation that still I miss her, after all this time, after all the pain." I put my head in my hands. My eyes felt hollow, strained and tired. How I longed to sleep.

"She chases me in my dreams," I sighed. "I'm not sure if I want her to catch me or not."

The world is broken, and I am broken with it. You have hunted me to the edge of despair and gloated at your power over me, mocked me while I wept in the corner, cowering in your presence. I run through the trees, colliding with branches, slipping on the wet leaves that litter the ground. I can feel you snapping at my ankles, hear you snarling behind me. My brain is on fire, in overload.

You have shown yourself to be the multi-headed serpent, the spectre of nightmare who takes many forms to deceive and to torture. She was your most successful performance. I see you reach for me with her hand, remember the feel of your fingers laced through mine.

I grip my head in my hands. The pressure inside my skull feels like my brain is going to explode. I scream into the rain, rage at the storm. Still I run from your growling and snarling. Every time I turn around, you are there, malevolent red eyes gleaming out of the dark.

Confusion pulls my addled mind in differing directions, stretching out my brain like it is mere plasticine. You enjoy the game, chuckle like a child making shapes with this stretchy, viscous matter, melting in the heat from the fire inside my skull, pulled thin into webs by your fingers.

Your fingers, her fingers. Interchangeable. You are now one and the same. I let you into my life, made love to your essence, your words; I craved your flesh and allowed you to defile and possess me. You were my world and you tore it down. You stole my heart and then you stole my dreams. I may have forgiven you for what you did, for the pain you caused, but I cannot forgive you for destroying my faith. You made me scared to love.

You sat back and watched as others plunged in the knife and then stepped forward to twist it. You ground me to dust, like a malevolent god crushing me in the palm of her hand. I loved you with all that I had and I gave you all that I could. Without you, I am a shell.

"No more!" I scream at the rain, at you behind me and before me. I can bear no more. There is so much heat and smoke in my head from the fire in my brain. The pressure builds; my brain may just snap. I collapse to my knees. My thoughts are a jumble. I clutch my head, the rain beating at my skull so hard that I can no longer draw breath under its might.

I hear the horn of an oncoming train. I stagger forward, crawling through the mud. I am sinking in it, drowning in it. I drag myself onward, feeling the metal of the train track, hearing the screech of the horn added to the shrill pitch of your screaming as you burn inside my skull, the fires of Hell reaching flashover, an explosion tearing through my mind.

My mind floats now, as if entirely detached from my body as it collapses across the rusted train track snaking through the forest. The train is bearing down on me, horn blaring and brakes squealing. I await the crush of metal, the mutilation of my body, the welcome pull of oblivion.

But it does not come. I open my eyes and watch the rain falling through the carcases of trees on to me, where I lie across a rusted old train track, abandoned. How I crave this silence. I want to escape, to get far away from everything. I want to go.

I look up to the old bridge beyond the trees. I have reached the edge of the forest, where the disused track veers off the main line that goes beneath the old bridge, leaving the town behind. Leaving both you and the darkness behind.

The rain hammers my exhausted head as I leave the trees. They push against me as I ascend the weathered steps to reach the top. I feel entirely disconnected, a refugee from the smoke and ashes of my rotten corpse, my fizzled brain that can take no more of your relentless prodding and tinkering; my body merely a shell, my mind like a floating cloud.

I gaze out to the distance, hear the whistling and the scraping of metal on metal. I clamber over the side, leaning forward, waiting for my moment to collide with fate.

I find that I can breathe more easily up here, tasting the rain on my lips like I did with you so long ago. I close my eyes, kissing your lips one last time, telling you that I love you, that I still love you even after all this time. There's someone else there too. Little Rosie, who surely can't be so little anymore.

"I love you, Dad."

I truly cannot say which is the greater of afflictions – living every day with the fear of loss, or when that fear becomes reality.

"I love you, too."

I let go, allowing the call of freedom to pull on my body.

From out of the night, a strong hand closes around my arm.

"Think of a time when you were irritated, wound-up by something or someone, how it gnaws away at you. Think of a time when you were fed up, dragged down by something, how heavy that feels. And you know when small children are running around you, screaming and shouting and full of the most exhausting and relentless energy, of which you don't even feel a fraction?

"Imagine all of those things at once, all of that noise, all together, ever-expanding simultaneously, dragging you further and further into a black hole, away from your ability to control the situation. That's what it's like inside my head, all the time. How I crave the silence, how I long for peace and calm."

Somewhere, I thought, I could hear a clock ticking. Counting down the moments of my life.

"Do you blame her, for where you came to tonight?"

I considered before answering. "No. What she did may have been the trigger, but we are all responsible for how we react, for how we manage our feelings. As impossible as that may be for me to do, it doesn't make anyone else responsible."

He nodded.

"What would you say to her, if you had the chance to finally confront her?"

I let the tears fall freely.

"That I forgive her. That I hope she's happy, finally happy. I obviously couldn't make her happy. I wasn't enough and that's okay. I don't wish her ill. She treated me badly, but that seems to be the constant cycle. The broken-hearted become the heartbreakers. Maybe in some sadistic way, they want to know how it feels to be the powerful one. It is the currency of the world."

"Do you want to feel that? To feel powerful?"

"Not if it means inflicting pain. Pain is a disease, the pandemic of the human condition."

I told him of my encounter with the homeless man. It felt so long ago now.

"I tend not to worry about the things I cannot control," he said. "If you can't control it, you shouldn't worry about it. If you can control it, then you've no need to worry."

"But that shouldn't be the same as not caring." I sank back in my seat, despondent. "It's easy to give up hope when you look at the world around us. Everyone wants to cut themselves off. There's no unity anymore, only division. Or perhaps there never has been unity. Countries on the brink of war, nations breaking apart from each other because they've forgotten the basic etiquette we teach to children – to share, to compromise, to develop in unity. We have the power to reach the greatest number of people with knowledge and understanding than we ever have before, yet we abuse it with greed and vanity and deception. The planet is burning; it crumbles and melts beneath our feet, but too many people would rather turn their heads away. We should be bowing them in shame."

Another news report flashed on the television screen, away from the burning rainforest.

"All we do is tear each other apart. A child goes missing every week. And this case – the media describes him as a serial killer."

"I'm not sure the term is accurate. There have only been two deaths."

"Don't you think there'll be more?"

He finished his tea.

"The media have dubbed him the 'Suicide Killer' – the victims didn't want to live."

"Does that make a difference?" I asked.

"You didn't want to live. There's more than one way to lend a helping hand."

I stared at him. He held my gaze.

"Forgive me, that was insensitive." He stood and placed a hand on my shoulder. "Another coffee?" He diverted towards the toilets on his way to the bar.

I finished my coffee, thinking of his helping hand, when he pulled me back from the edge of the bridge. What if that hand had pushed me the other way, rather than pulling me back?

I was gripped from behind, material pressed over my mouth. I felt the room swim, lips pressed close to my ear as I sank.

"You were the perfect patient."

230

I hear my own shallow breathing in the pitch blackness, struggling to draw each breath, burning in my chest. I try hard to think through the process, but cannot focus, my mind ranging from shaky image to blurred recollection to blank moment, like old video footage playing on tattered film.

Blood runs between my fingers as I scrape and hit at the wood above and surrounding me, my accompanying screams long dead in my scratched, dry throat. My projected safety of a cabin deep in the woods has shrunk to the reality of my coffin in a shallow grave.

There are moments when you still chase me through the forest. Still I hear the pattering of rainfall. You will follow me always, with your many faces and deceptions. I met another of your faces today, he with the helping hand, saving me only to use me as his puppet, dragging my half-conscious body through the fire escape behind us and bundling me into the boot of a car outside. The careful planning of an expert. Do I make it to three?

I woke here, confused, blind, the sounds of pouring rain and shovelling earth above my head, thumping against the wood. In the end, you were the victor. As you always are.

You are the monster stalking the streets, the killer whispering in our ears. You tell us that we are worthless, that the world and everyone we love are better off without us. You are the demon that possesses our souls. We are desperate, sinking in desolation. You tell us that we shouldn't go on.

You are a liar.

You hunt me still. I can hear it all around me, the scuffling and scraping. Laboured breath. Someone – or something – is here with me. You have finally caught up with me. I hear your fingers scraping at the wood, mere inches from me.

A face flashes into my mind. My lips are moving, soundless. I cannot form words. Cannot say the name. Memory fails me.

I hear scraping above my head, like the earth is being clawed away from my tomb. Scavengers have caught up with me and eagerly seek their meal beneath the earth. But I can no longer breathe, can no longer feel my hands scraping at the knotted wood. Perhaps our entire life is preparation, leading to the final battle. A battle we have no hope of winning.

The sudden explosion of light is blinding, engulfing what remains of my consciousness; consuming…overpowering…

Is this how it feels to be free?

Also by Lee Allen

THE JACK O'LANTERN MEN

Hear our words. Say your prayers.

Late on Hallowe'en night, Frank is delivered to the
Jailer, standing accused of a crime for which he will
hang. He has a tale to tell, and begs the Jailer to
speak to his daughter.

His daughter, Laura, has her own tale to tell.
Through their words, the Jailer hears of the events
that will lead him to his last execution.

All the while, the Jack O'Lantern Men wait in the
wings for the last act to play out and the curtain to
fall.

"An intense read…cleverly written…"
Amazon Kindle Reader

"A gripping horror story with an unexpected twist."
Goodreads Reader

"Gripping story line…couldn't put the book
down…"
Amazon Kindle Reader

Also by Lee Allen

ALONE

All things must end.

Recovering from a recent accident and faced with the prospect of spending another Christmas alone, Jessica accepts the invitation of an old flame to spend Christmas with him and his aged aunt at his manor house in the midst of the Brecon Beacons.

Feeling her arrival is unwelcome, Jessica awaits her reunion with a face from the past, while a snowstorm postpones his arrival and renders her trapped within the house. Behind the silence, something dark is lurking.

Left with little choice, Jessica finds she must face the secrets the old house hides. Yet what she may come to learn is that nothing haunts us more than the secrets of our own pasts, and that burying them does not make them forgotten.

"Couldn't put it down."
Amazon Kindle Reader

"Tenderly written with a satisfying twist."
Goodreads Reader

"Left me feeling incredibly emotional…[the] writing style is beautiful…[a] fantastic book."
"A Daily Cloud" Review Blog

Also by Lee Allen

THOSE CRIMES OF PASSION

We are all capable of the most unimaginable things.
But many of us never find out what they are.

A school is locked in an atmosphere of unease and suspicion, and a young woman is brutally raped by a dangerous assailant. But events are soon to spiral out of control for Jennifer Kraystone and her friend Jonathan Baker. Caught in a web of crime and corruption, they are finding they can truly trust no one, while finally embracing the feelings they have denied themselves for so long.

But as their lives rip apart, can their growing passion protect them through all they must face, or will it ultimately threaten to corrupt their relationship with tragedy?

"Thrilling and terrifying…not to be read alone…"
Amazon Kindle Reader

"Not for the faint hearted."
Lulu.com Reader

"Keeps you guessing and in suspense until the very end."
Amazon Kindle Reader